Cerulean Sky

Cerulean Sky

David Corse

POLYMATH
— PRESS —

Aurora, CO

Cerulean Sky by David Corse

This book is a work of fiction. All incidents, events, characters, names, businesses, places, and other entities depicted are either fictitious or are used fictitiously.

Copyright © 2025 by the author.

Cover art and layout by Nichole Bosso.
Interior design by Robert Lewis.
Author photo by Sarah Klenakis.

All rights reserved. No portion of this book may be reproduced in any form without written permission from the publisher or copyright holder.

Published by Polymath Press, a trade name of Polymath Enterprises, LLC. Please direct all inquiries to Polymath Press, P. O. Box 461870, Aurora, CO 80046-1870, online at www.polymathpress.com, or via email to editor@polymathpress.com.

First edition

November, 2025

ISBN (trade paperback): 978-1-961827-14-1
ISBN (eBook): 978-1-961827-15-8
Library of Congress Control Number: 2025946149

To my wife.
Thank you for marrying me and the
imaginary people in my head.

Also by David Corse

"Mother is Coming Home" in *Split Scream Volume Six* (Tenebrous Press, 2025)

Praise for *Cerulean Sky*

"*Cerulean Sky* takes you on a heart-wrenching journey that's equal parts romantic and disturbing. Corse throws his characters into a deadly preternatural world, and dares readers not to get attached. Fans of adult-oriented, dystopian literature don't want to miss this book."

- **Lauren Bolger**, author of *The Barre Incidents* and *Kill Radio*

"Cerulean Sky will break you in the best way possible. David Corse writes big characters with big emotions that you'll want to come back to again and again. If you want horror, romance, and action, this book is for you."

- **Alex Woodroe**, author of *Whisperwood* and Editor-In-Chief of Tenebrous Press

"I dare you not to choke up reading Cerulean Sky. David Corse's dystopian story is a heady mix of dark fantasy, romance, and action. You'll love Corse's characters— even when you hate their decisions."

-**Michael Bettendorf**, author of *Trve Cvlt*

Chapter One

Florence tugs at her elbow-length gloves. It's a soupy ninety-five degrees outside and the sweat trapped within her protective coverings agitates her skin. "I'm roasting," she grumbles at her boyfriend, Peter. "Remind me why we're here."

Peter flashes her a too-wide smile that shows a comical number of teeth. "Because you love me," he says in a tone that's halfway to a question. Florence smirks. His excitement is almost strong enough to make her forget that she's outside and not safe at home.

"The jury's still deliberating," she says. "But there's hope."

The pair are at the entrance to Forgotten Treasures, a monthly flea market held in a school parking lot near their apartment. A dozen white canopy tents dot the blacktop at odd intervals. Thirty or forty shoppers wander the market, and the sight of so many people in one place makes Florence's stomach fold into itself.

A white sun-beaten A-frame sign blocks the entrance like a bored sentry. Florence reads it, though she knows what it says. Signs like it are everywhere people gather.

SOLOMON'S DISEASE PROTOCOLS ENFORCED
Protective clothing required
Obey social distancing
Do not touch others
FORGOTTEN TREASURES IS NOT RESPONSIBLE FOR YOUR SAFETY

Someone has drawn a crude stick figure with outstretched arms on the left side of the sign. Next to it is a speech bubble that says, "Can I get a hug?" Florence grimaces at the morbid joke. One-hundred million people have died from Solomon's in the last five years—her mother among them. She still remembers the anxiety she felt when she learned it was spread by skin-to-skin contact.

Why did I agree to this? She asks herself, and then immediately offers a rebuttal. *Peter needs this. It makes him happy, and happiness is rare in the End Times. You can be strong for him.*

Looking over at Peter, she can't help but love him. He's kind and funny, though sometimes overprotective. She loves his singing voice and the songs he writes her while squirreled away in their one-bedroom apartment. Most of his music is melancholy, but he isn't above strumming out a goofy nonsense song and the occasional love song just for the two of them. Florence has had her fair share of boyfriends, and Peter is the best of them all.

Rolling her shoulders to ease the tension in her back, she reminds herself Forgotten Treasures isn't an orgy of naked flesh. The people who shop here are cautious. "Excited?" she asks.

"I've been ready for a decade."

A week ago, Dan, Peter's friend who collects and sells records on the side, found a rare album by The Midnight Provisionists, Peter's favorite band and the inspiration for his own music. The record, according to Peter, is "a once-in-a-lifetime find." The timing of Dan's discovery couldn't have been more perfect. Florence was starting to worry about Peter's mental health. He said he was spending long sleepless nights contemplating the velocity of the world's decline.

"After you," Florence says and sweeps her hands forward.

"Of course." He adjusts his black protective gloves and whips a black hood over his messy brown hair. His angular face disappears into half shadow, and for a brief moment Florence thinks he looks like a cross between the Grim Reaper and a rock star.

Here we go, Florence thinks and absently rubs at her own annoying silver gloves. Peter strolls past the warning sign, but before Florence can follow, he spins around to face her and juts his hands to both sides. He wiggles his fingers for dramatic effect. "See? Nothing to worry about. Completely safe."

Despite Florence not telling him about her fears, Peter must have sensed them. She might joke that the jury in charge of her heart is still deliberating, but there isn't a bigger lie. There was never any deliberation. Florence knew she loved Peter on their third date. His reassurance saps the fear from her body. Where it goes, Florence doesn't care. Three quick steps carry her past the sign and into the market.

"After this, we'll go home and turn the air conditioner to Arctic and freeze ourselves into popsicles," Peter says. "I promise."

"We better," Florence replies.

Dan's stall is in the back. Taking the lead, Peter cuts through the crowd, giving each person more than the CDC-recommended eight feet of distance. When they're almost to the stall, a joyous laugh catches Florence's attention. Along the edge of the market, a young girl with a long ponytail rides her bike down the sidewalk.

Florence freezes at the sight. Unlike everyone else, the girl is wearing shorts and a T-shirt, a deadly combination that exposes her skin on her arms and legs to the disease. But this isn't the only reason Florence stops. The girl's soft circular face and sleepy eyes are familiar. She is the very image of Nancy, Florence's childhood best friend.

"Earth to Flo, are you there?" Peter asks.

Florence startles and drags an arm up to point at the little girl. "Sorry, I'm here. I can't believe someone hasn't called the DPF. It's so dangerous."

Peter makes a noncommittal grunt. "I'm sure her parents are around. Let's keep going."

Dan's Earworm Records is four rows of vinyl under sagging white canvas. Short and round with skinny legs, Dan is an aging rocker. He has on his ever-present denim vest that's loaded with pins and patches. "Are you ready for magic?" Dan calls out as Peter and Florence approach.

Peter waves and speeds up. At the same time, Florence slows. She can't get the little girl out of her mind. "Go ahead. I'll be right there," she says to Peter, who turns and raises an eyebrow at her but keeps moving.

A dark mood settles over Florence as she faces the little girl on the bike. Nancy died twenty years ago, but the wound in Florence's heart is still fresh. She misses her more and more every day. While watching, Florence rubs her forearms again. Her hands are suffocating inside her protective gloves. She lets out an annoyed groan and peeks around to see if other shoppers are nearby. Peter and Dan are closest. *Make it quick*, she tells herself. Yanking her lefthand glove off, Florence sighs in relief. Sweat covers her forearms and drips to the asphalt.

"Yuck," she says as she wipes her palm and wrist on her shirt.

A loud bang cuts through the market and Florence's mouth goes dry with fear. A cacophony of screams follows. They're coming from her left, from the heart of the market. Florence wheels around, searching for Peter. She spots him on the far side of the record stall and tracks his gaze to the location of the noise.

"Out of the way!" A terrified voice booms from somewhere in the middle of the crowd. People shriek and dive for cover. A haggard-looking naked man with milk-pale skin and a yellow-orange glow emanating off his body lopes in Florence's direction. With each step, he bounces a little too high and floats for a quarter of a second. It's like gravity doesn't exist for him.

He's infected, Florence screams in her mind. But she doesn't move. Her legs are stone—no, they are mountains. They have stood here, where Florence stands now, for millennia and will stand for millennia more. Florence squeezes her eyes shut. *I'm going to die—just like Mom.*

Then her Peter is there, at her side, forcing her to move, pulling the mountain from the earth with supernatural strength. "Run!" he shouts and leads them toward the girl on the bike, away from the dying man, Solomon's next victim.

Florence takes a half-dozen steps before she realizes she's dropped her glove. "I need to go back."

"Forget it," Peter says and drags her away.

Over her shoulder, Florence sees the haggard man pivot in their direction. A man to Florence's left cries out in terror and stammers "Please, Jesus" over and over. Eager to escape, the praying man runs wild and, in his fear, slams into Florence, ripping her away from Peter. The panicked crowd fills the space between them, and the last thing Florence sees is his calloused outstretched hand.

"Don't let him touch you!" a woman with short gray hair shouts. She's ten, maybe fifteen feet, behind the haggard man. Unbelievably, she's sprinting at him. Next to the woman is a square-jawed young man with close-cropped hair and a muscular build. Both wear vests emblazoned with the DPF insignia across the front. Their guns are drawn.

Florence knows what the agents' presence means. The haggard man is a runner. And the Disease Protection Force's policy on runners is simple and immutable: execute on sight.

"Flo, here!" Peter shouts. He's made his way far past the little girl, who to Florence's horror, has climbed off her bike to watch the commotion. A wide smile is etched on the girl's face, like this is the best TV show she's ever seen.

Florence heads toward the girl, shouting for her to run, to hide, to never come back outside again. But the little girl doesn't listen; she's motionless, mouth agape. Florence is skin and bones, and she's uncertain if she can carry the little girl, but she has to try.

As she closes in on the child, Florence's right sneaker snags on a crack in the asphalt and she slams into the hard ground. The side of her head thuds against the concrete and her vision blurs. A rich, metallic taste fills her mouth as blood rolls off her bottom lip and down her chin.

She blinks several times in rapid succession and shakes her head to focus. The little girl is less than ten feet away in the same spot she was in before Florence fell. Behind her, Florence hears the haggard man approaching. Looking back, she catches his gaze. He's wild with fear.

"Get out of here," Florence shrieks at the girl and waves an arm at her to shoo her away. This time Florence's words stick. The little girl struggles onto her bike, catches her balance, and pedals hard. For a half a heartbeat, it looks like she's going to turn her handlebars left or right and ride off to play someplace else. But she doesn't. The girl pedals toward Florence and the runner.

A surprised gasp tumbles out of the haggard man as he pivots to avoid crashing into the girl and her exposed skin. Off balance, he staggers toward Florence.

I need to move, Florence thinks, but it's already too late.

The runner plows into Florence, falling on top of her. On instinct, she shoves him hard, trying desperately to push the man away, to protect herself, to live. "Get off! Get off! Don't touch me!"

"I'm sorry. I'm so, so sorry," the haggard man says as he climbs to his feet. "I didn't touch your skin! I swear!" He looks over his shoulder, sees the two DPF agents, and flees.

Florence stays on the blacktop, too terrified to move. None of this is real, she tells herself. All she wants is to be back at her apartment with Peter, enjoying the air conditioner and watching Netflix. Why did she agree to go outside today? Why is she here?

"Did he touch you?" It's the woman DPF agent. She looms over Florence, brow furrowed in concern. When Florence doesn't answer, the woman growls in annoyance and points at her partner. "Jake, she's yours," she says and sprints after the runner.

"On it, Erin," Jack barks back.

The square-jawed young officer points his pistol at Florence and her bowels drop. She knows it's loaded with rubber bullets to prevent blood splatter, but the weapon is still terrifying. "Did he touch you?" he asks in a commanding voice.

Florence slides her ungloved hand behind her back to hide it, but the motion captures the agent's attention.

"Show me your hands!"

Shrinking into herself, she slowly raises her arms above her head. "I don't know," she stammers. Panic grips her as the worst-case scenario runs through her mind. If the haggard man touched her exposed skin…she's infected.

She's dead.

"Doesn't matter now," Jake says. "I'm authorized to use deadly force on runners." A long pause follows and Jake's gun dips slightly. He stares her in the eyes, and Florence realizes that he's younger than she is. Probably not even thirty yet. "Don't be a runner."

Florence shakes her head but doesn't speak. She has no words. Everything is happening too quickly.

Jake raises a palm in a placating gesture. It does nothing to stop Florence's rapid heartbeat. "That's good. I'm going to hel—"

A guttural scream cuts Jack's words short. Peter rushes the agent, an aluminum baseball bat held high. He strikes the man on the top of his shoulder and the agent crumbles to his knees, dazed. Gripping the bat like a spear, Peter slams the barrel into the side of Jake's head, and he collapses unconscious to the asphalt.

It takes a moment for Florence's brain to process the scene. A mixture of fear and anger overtakes her. "What did you do?" she shout-cries.

"Get up," Peter answers in a breathless rush. He's filled with kinetic motion, bouncing on his toes as he whips his head from side to side. "We have to go."

"I can't." She doesn't want to be a runner. She doesn't want a rubber bullet in the back and a lethal dart in the chest.

"They're going to come for you."

"What if I'm not infected?" Florence counters as she rises to her feet and smears the blood off her chin with her remaining glove. Every muscle in her body is tight with fear. "Why did you hit him?"

Peter narrows his eyes and jabs the bat at the prone agent. "He had a gun in your face!"

Florence clutches her shirt. This was all an accident, a misunderstanding. They can fix this.

"Get out of here!" someone yells. As Florence twists toward the voice, something heavy hits her shoulder, forcing her to back up. More shocking than painful, she hisses at the impact. A short woman with braided hair stands at the center of a loose crowd of shoppers. Florence recognizes her. She sells handmade jams. A jar explodes at Florence's feet and sprays her shoes with sticky blue jelly.

"Runner!" someone else calls out.

"No—I'm not a runner!" Florence shouts back. Something hard hits her on the side of her face. It's a white decorative candle.

A man moves for Jake's gun and Peter leaps at him, his bat held high. "Try it!" The man blanches and skitters away.

Peter kicks the gun behind him, away from the crowd. "Flo, we have to leave right now."

She knows he's right. If they stay, the crowd will pelt

them to death. She whirls around until she spots the little girl on the bike; she's maneuvered in front of the crowd and stands partially mounted.

"Go home," Florence says. "Go home and don't come back outside."

Chapter Two

Florence bursts through the door to her apartment and throws herself into the shower with her clothes still on. Frigid water blasts her face, but she barely notices. She squirts soap on her forearm and rubs it vigorously. When she realizes the water isn't warm, she twists the knob and yelps in pain as scalding liquid hammers her body. Eventually, she manages to adjust the water to a temperature that's less than blistering.

"Please, please, please," Florence whispers as she works. This isn't how things are supposed to happen. She has years ahead of her, things she wants to do, places she wants to visit. She's never even been to California, much less Europe.

Florence peels off her shirt, bra, and remaining glove. She methodically cleans every inch of her of her arms and chest. She slips and falls as she tries to remove her linen pants, and instead of standing back up, stays at the bottom of the tub. The soap goes fast. When it's gone, she uses shampoo.

"We have to hurry," Peter says from the doorway. "We can't stay here." He rushes off into the apartment.

Slowly, Florence staggers from the shower and wraps her arms around her stomach. She tells herself to calm down, to breathe. She tells herself that everything will work out. She's one of the lucky ones. She knows it. She has to be. Otherwise....

"Five minutes," Peter calls from the bedroom. "That's all the time we have. Grab whatever you can."

When Florence doesn't leave the bathroom, Peter flings the door fully open and claps his hands repeatedly to get her attention. Florence stiffens in surprise. "Flo, please, we have to hurry, okay?" He places a pair of jeans, a blue shirt, and a pair of black gloves on the ground in front of her. "Put these on."

Florence hesitates before tugging her clothes on. "Why do we need to leave? Maybe it didn't take. We don't know." She follows him into their bedroom.

Peter tosses a duffle bag on their bed and shoves clothing inside indiscriminately. "I attacked a DPF agent. And you...you might be infected. You ran. You're a runner. They kill runners."

"But they don't know where we live. They don't know our names. The DPF agent barely saw me. He won't remember my face. We don't have to leave." She glances around the bedroom. It's small and cozy, just like the rest of their apartment. She's lived here for almost four years.

It's home—the only place she's felt connected to since she was a little girl.

Peter shakes his head. He stops shoving things into the bag long enough to look Florence in the eyes. He's just as freaked out as she is. "Dan knows my name. He has my phone number. He saw everything. Flo, the DPF isn't stupid. They're going to find out who I am, and then they're going to find out who you are. And if we aren't careful, they're going to kill us both."

Florence's legs turn to jelly, and she collapses onto the mattress. Peter stares at her, worry etched in his face, and then tosses her a tattered gray backpack. He doesn't say a word. He doesn't need to. She knows Peter is right. They need to run. She forces herself to stand and fills the bag.

♦ ♦ ♦

Once outside the apartment complex, Peter leads them to their decade-old sedan that's parked in front of the building. He drops into the driver's seat and turns the engine over before Florence reaches the front passenger door. The door squeals as she opens it.

"Hey, stop," Peter says forcefully. "Sit in the back."

Startled by Peter's tone, she flings herself away from the vehicle and into the busy street. A passing car blares its horn. She yelps and jump-walks back to the car. Her entire body feels twitchy, like she drank a pot of coffee on an empty stomach.

Peter is out of the car and staring at her over the roof.

"You okay?"

I'm not, she thinks. *I might never be again.* Instead of replying, she waves him off and closes the door with a flick of her wrist. It squeals louder this time. She hates the noise. It's like having a pin driven into her ear. She always meant to get it fixed, but never got around it to it. It'll probably never happen now.

"I'm sorry," Peter says, not look at her. "It's too dangerous for us to sit next to each other. You might accidentally touch me and then I'd be...." He trails off. He doesn't need to finish the sentence.

Peter's words drive spikes through Florence's already frayed nerves. If she infected Peter through her carelessness, she'd never forgive herself. She doesn't want to be responsible for another person's death. "Right, yeah. It's the safe play." She tosses her bag onto the back seat and climbs in. Peter situates himself behind the steering wheel. She's barely settled before the vehicle accelerates into traffic.

"Yes!" Peter howls and slaps the steering wheel. "I didn't think we'd make it!" His voice is adrenaline-fueled and higher than normal, the way he sounds after he's played an especially good set. He doesn't relax, but his shoulders uncoil.

Florence wishes she felt the same. Instead, a hot bubble of acid creeps to the back of her throat and she can't stop shaking. They've escaped the DPF but not the disease. Not yet anyway. Squeezing her eyes shut, she recalls everything she knows about Solomon's.

Being touched by someone with the disease isn't an

explicit death sentence. Blessed Ones, Walking Miracles, Anomalies, there are dozens of names for people who've been touched by an infected person and survived. She just has to wait. Signs of infection appear within twenty hours of exposure. It starts with the hands. They'll glow faintly and turn immaterial. And if she is infected, she has four days before she disintegrates into motes of preternatural light.

"Flo, talk to me," Peter says. He's looking at her through the rear-view mirror, one eyebrow raised.

She shakes her head. She doesn't want to talk. It's all too much to take in. Too much to process. He wants her to be excited that they escaped, but she's not. All she feels is afraid.

A block from the apartment, Florence feels a nagging sensation in the back of her mind that she forgot something. It's possible. Probably likely. They were moving so fast. She runs through a mental checklist and comes up blank. Anything and everything that's important to her is in the faded gray backpack by her side. But the thought lingers.

Florence pulls the backpack toward her and spills its contents on the seat. There's clothing and jewelry, and cash inside a small metal tin that she kept hidden in the back of her closet.

"What?" Peter asks.

"It's not here," she says, panic rising. She knows she packed Nancy's picture. She'd never forget it. It'd be like losing part of herself. "I have to go back."

Peter turns to look at her and nearly swerves off the

road. "No—we're not going back. It's too late. Whatever you forgot, it can't be that important. It just can't."

Florence pounds on the seat in front of her and glares out the window. She's not leaving the picture behind. She doesn't care what Peter thinks. She grips the door handle and takes a deep breath. This is going to hurt. She flings open the car door and prepares to jump. They aren't going that fast. She should walk away with only a few bruises.

"Shit, Flo!" Peter shouts and slams the brakes. The car skids to a stop.

"Wait for me!" She launches herself out of the car and sprints up the block.

Her lungs are burning by the time she reaches her apartment building. She hasn't run this fast since high school gym class, and if she's honest with herself, not even then. She was always a fifteen-minute mile type of girl.

Florence takes the stairs two at a time, plows into her third-floor walk-up, and beelines to the bedroom. With a surge of adrenaline, she yanks open her dresser's top drawer and searches for Nancy's picture. All she sees are old keepsakes, old Valentine's Day cards, a ceramic turtle the size of her palm, and her grandfather's Aviator sunglasses. What she doesn't see is her diary. She keeps Nancy's picture tucked inside so it doesn't get creased.

This doesn't make sense, she thinks. If it isn't in this drawer, or the car, she doesn't know where it would be.

On the verge of tears, she jerks out the remaining drawers and tips them out. Her diary and the picture aren't there either. In desperation, she checks Peter's drawers. Nothing.

"Where are you?" She runs her gloved fingers through her wet hair. She knows for certain she pulled her diary out of the drawer to pack it. *It has to be in this room.* Dropping to her hands and knees, Florence searches under her side of the bed and starts to cry when she spots a black and white composition notebook. Nancy's picture pokes out one side.

"Thank God," Florence utters as she snatches up the notebook. She kisses the cover and then holds it to her forehead. Without the picture, she's scared she might forget what Nancy looked like.

She's still hugging the notebook when the faint sound of sirens catches her attention. Jumping to her feet, she listens harder. It's a big city. The sirens might not be for her. There are emergencies every second of every day. The sirens grow louder, and icy fear runs down her spine. Peter was right, there wasn't enough time for her to come back. The DPF found her.

Florence dashes from her apartment. She makes it down one flight before she hears unfamiliar voices. Holding her breath, she peeks over the railing. Two heads bob up and down on the stairwell. She doesn't know if it's Jake and his partner. But it doesn't matter. If the agents see her, they will try to kill her. Her mind flashes to the lethal dart guns they carry to execute runners. They're supposed to be humane. Nothing is humane about them now. She needs to hide, and she needs to do it quickly.

Each floor is divided into a left and right unit. She tries the door on her left, but it doesn't budge. The unit on the right is also locked. *Calm down*, she tells herself. She knows the woman who lives in the 2R. Her name is Mrs. Jonston, and Florence watched her cats for a weekend a few years ago. She keeps a spare key in the potted plants outside her door.

Florence searches the plants and finds the key inside a pink watering can. She unlocks the door and slips inside. Trembling, she gently closes the door and twist the lock shut. *Keep going*, she thinks at the agents. *One more flight and you're there.*

"What the hell is going on?" a woman says from behind her. The voice belongs to Mrs. Jonston.

"Stay back," Florence almost shouts. She rounds on the old woman and shoots a hand out, fingers splayed.

Mrs. Jonston tilts her head and takes a tiny step back, and then her face sags with concern. "You don't look good, Florence."

Through the door, Florence hears heavy footfalls, and then shouting from above, but she can't make out what the agents are saying. Her bladder is near to exploding.

"I'm sorry," Florence says in a panic. The woman's day is going to be ruined when the agents discover Florence hid in her apartment. "I really am." She unlocks the door and sneaks into the hallway.

Her legs feel like lead, but she keeps pushing and almost stumbles down the steps twice, catching herself on the handrail each time. She expects to hear Mrs. Jonston shout to the agents, but the old woman doesn't. Florence doesn't know if the woman is protecting her or if she's in shock.

A hot stitch runs up Florence's right side and she slows to a sad jog. Half a block ahead of her, Peter is leaning out the car window, urging her forward. Seeing her slowing, he recedes back into the car and reverses down the block like a reckless bowling ball. Florence is barely moving and covered in a thick layer of sweat when Peter jerks to a stop next to her.

"I hope it was worth it," he says as Florence falls inside the vehicle.

It was.

Chapter Three

The yellow light in the filthy motel bathroom flickers and hums. Florence's head pounds. She sits on the tile floor, legs pulled to her chest, arms wrapped around her knees. She squeezes her eyes shut, breathes deeply, and leans her back against a pale pink bathtub. It's been fifteen hours since the haggard man touched her. Another five and she's in the clear.

She shifts, trying and failing to get comfortable, and focuses on her hands. If she's infected, her hands will be the first part of her body to betray her. She opens and closes them, balling them into tight fists. Not a single thing is wrong with them; they are her hands, with the same bony fingers her mother once said would be good for playing piano. They feel the same as they did that morning in the market, the same as they felt an hour ago.

I might get through this, she thinks. She's had this same

thought a thousand times, and it's always followed by its negative. *What if I'm infected?* Her mind is a rollercoaster, and it's exhausting.

Florence has been locked inside the motel bathroom for four hours, but it feels like years. After her escape, Peter took the highway west toward New York and Pennsylvania. That's where their smartphones are, in the weeds along a nameless highway. They drove at a snail's pace, worried their aging car would pop a tire from the deteriorating highway. When they got far enough away from the city, they stopped at an ATM to pull as much money as they could from their meager bank accounts. Then Peter filled the gas tank, and as a backup purchased a five-gallon gas can and filled it too.

After nightfall, Peter became too tired to drive. He pulled off the highway and together they searched for a safe place to spend the night. An hour of hunting led them to Silver Lake Motel, a grungy one-story motor lodge that looked on the verge of going out of business. In their headlights, Florence could see that the structure was a dingy sky blue with weathered plywood over half the windows. She'd never stay at the motel under normal circumstances. But these weren't normal circumstance.

Peter paid for the room in cash while Florence waited in the car. When it was time to go inside, he propped open the room's door and she bolted to the bathroom to quarantine. It's where she's been since, counting the hours on a small digital clock. She saw it sitting on a bedside table when she rushed into the bathroom and asked Peter to bring it to her not long after they arrived. She hates how slow it tells time. It's not a logical thought, but it's honest.

A knock at the door snaps Florence into the present. She gives her hands another squeeze. *Stay this way,* she thinks at them. *Don't be infected.* She drags her eyes away and turns them to the locked door. Peter is on the other side. "Yes?"

"I brought you something to eat."

"Wait." Her protective gloves are neatly folded and rest on top of her zipped backpack. She tugs the gloves on and, with a heavy groan, climbs to her feet. "Set it on the floor and step back."

She waits for Peter to move to the opposite side of the room and then cracks open the door. An odd pile of food from the motel's vending machine sits on the carpet in front of her: a chocolate bar, bright orange peanut butter crackers, and, surprisingly, a disposable cup filled with steaming instant Ramen. Her stomach turns at the sight of it all. "I'm not hungry."

"Try to eat something, please."

"Maybe later."

This is the first time she's seen Peter since he gave her the digital clock. His face is gaunt from exhaustion and dark circles hang under his eyes. He looks strung out and on the verge of collapse. She knows he slept for an hour, maybe two, when they arrived, but since then, he's been a sentinel, checking on her every hour, trying to coax her out of her depressions, to encourage her to believe in their future.

"You should come out," Peter says. "We can watch TV. It might take your mind off things. *Little Shop of Hor-*

rors is on. The remake with Rick Moranis. You love that movie."

Florence shakes her head. "It's safer this way."

"I can stay on one side of the room. You can stay on the other."

Again, she shakes her head. "I'm going to stay in the bathroom." Peter sighs and rubs his eyes, obviously frustrated that he can't help more. If he could, he'd fight all her battles for her, she thinks. "Get some rest, please."

She starts to back into the bathroom, but Peter takes a tentative step forward and crosses his arms. She knows his body language intimately. He wants to talk, and it's serious.

"Wait," he says.

Florence leans her entire body against the doorframe, almost like she's hugging it. "What is there to talk about?"

"Everything. We need a plan. We can't go from motel to motel. We probably shouldn't be here. People have eyes, Flo. They're paranoid. You should have seen the way the night manager looked at me. He didn't want to take our money. He *needed* to."

I should have been more paranoid, Florence laments. To Peter, she says, "Not yet." What she doesn't add is their choices are limited. If she's infected, it won't matter where she goes. Even if she's one of the Blessed Ones, they'll still be on the run from the DPF. Their old life is gone.

She starts to close the door again and Peter takes another step toward her. In a panicked voice he calls out, "I'll protect you. You know that, right? No matter what. I'm not going anywhere. Even if you're—"

"Don't say it," Florence says quickly.

"There are places where we can be happy."

She wants that too, infected or not. "Sleep. Promise me."

Peter nods, but she doesn't believe him.

For the third time, Florence attempts to close the bathroom door and succeeds. Once she's situated on the tile again, she removes her gloves, folds them, and places them back on top of her pack. Both of her hands are the same as they were a few minutes ago. Still strong, still solid.

More time passes. Long, excruciating minutes. Torturous hours. At 3:42 a.m., she stifles a yawn and thinks back to the last time she stayed up this late. It was the night she and Nancy made vision boards in her parents' basement and watched *Titanic* on a beat-up VHS player.

Stretching across the bathroom floor, Florence drags her backpack to her and rummages through it until she finds her diary. It's filled with drawings, short, rambling entries, and half-finished apology letters to Nancy's mother, Mrs. Barnes.

Nancy's picture is sandwiched in the middle of the notebook between two blank pages. Carefully, Florence removes the pictures. The left corner is bent. It must have happened when she escaped the DPF at her apartment. She does her best to smooth the dogear, but the crease is permanent. It should be framed, Florence knows, but she's always resisted the idea. You frame pictures you want to display, and Florence doesn't want to show the world this photo. She doesn't want questions. She doesn't want to have to explain.

In the picture, Florence and Nancy sit on a log, hugging each other. They are thirteen, gangly and awkward, with their hair pulled back in messy ponytails. They look like sisters, and in a sense they were. Mrs. Barnes took the picture of them a few weeks before her daughter drowned.

It was Florence's fault.

Florence touches the picture and tears up. It doesn't matter that she's seen the image countless times, it still stirs a painful mix of sadness and shame inside her. Hatred too—hatred of herself and what she did.

"I should have listened to you," she says. "I'm sorr—"

Hot pain explodes in Florence's stomach, and she doubles over. Her insides feel like they're burning. She tries to call for Peter, but her lungs aren't working, and only unintelligible gasps cross her lips.

Like a serpent made of dancing flame, the pain winds into her chest. Florence arches her back against the bathtub and slaps at her solar plexus in a useless attempt to stop the agony under her skin. When the burning reaches the middle of her chest, it splits in two. Each hate-filled flame rolls slowly down her bicep, across the crook of her elbow, and past her wrist. Here the pain subsides for a half a breath before coming back worse than before. Her hands lock into claws as the fire reaches her palms. But the pain doesn't stop. It presses on. Her fingertips burn like she's pressed them against a blazing hot cast-iron skillet. A dim, yellow-orange light pulses under the skin of her right forearm and her flesh feels like it wants to peel itself from her bones.

She doesn't know how long the pain lasts, but when it finally dissipates, she's laying on her side sobbing. She sucks air into her tired lungs and pushes herself up so she's sitting again.

The bathroom doorknob rattles. Heavy pounding bows the cheap pressed wood. "Flo, what's happening? Unlock the door! Let me in!"

Florence trembles. "I'm fine," she whispers to herself. "I'm fine. I'm fine. I'm fine. Nothing is wrong."

Nancy's picture is on the tile next to her. She must have dropped it. As she reaches for it, a lone tremor rumbles through her body. An aftershock, she thinks. As she tries to pick up the picture, she feels a slight pressure in her pointer finger, and in disbelief stares as her entire hand passes effortlessly through the picture and floor tile. She quickly yanks her hand back and balls it into a fist.

Then she wails.

Chapter Four

Florence flings open the bathroom door, and Peter scrambles away. He makes it a few feet before he trips and slams into the filthy beige carpet. They lock eyes and understanding passes between them—Florence is infected.

"I…I…I can't breathe," Florence stammers. Sweat pours down her forehead. She feels like the motel room is collapsing on her. She needs to get out, to leave this room, to run. She stumbles to the door and tries to grab the knob but her traitorous right hand passes through it. She feels nothing when it happens except for the odd pressure she felt when the same hand passed through Nancy's picture. She tries again and again to grab the knob, but her hand passes through it each time.

Somewhere behind her she hears Peter rise to his feet. "Flo, please, talk to me."

She doesn't want to talk. She doesn't want to think.

Groaning, she attempts to open the door with her left hand. For a heartbeat, she thinks this hand has also betrayed her. But it hasn't. The metal knob is cool against her palm. She jerks the door open and lurches into the night.

The motel's parking lot stretches out before her, illuminated by harsh white lights mounted above each room's door. Their car is to her left, the night manager's office to her right. The man is watching TV and laughing loudly. Beyond the parking lot is a shallow drainage ditch filled with stinking brown water and litter. Past this is the nameless two-lane road they came in on.

Florence's feet carry her forward. She doesn't pick a direction on purpose. She just needs to move, to flee. In the back of her mind, she knows what she's doing is useless, but she's listening to her heart. And her heart is screaming for her to run; it's telling her that if she never stops, she'll never die.

Feet pound the pavement behind her. "Wait!" Peter calls out, but Florence doesn't listen. When she reaches the end of the parking lot, she pushes onto the grass that leads to the drainage ditch and then slides down it. She splashes through the foul-smelling water, climbs out of the ditch, and barrels into the road.

Just keep going, Florence thinks. *Just keep walking. You'll be—*

A car horn blares behind her, and she shrieks in surprise. She spins around, and two bright lights blind her. In a panic, she jumps to the side and tumbles down the drainage ditch into the filthy water. She barely has time to register what happened before Peter appears at the top of the trench, eyes wide with fear. The very sight of him pisses her off.

"Why'd you make me go there?" Florence shouts. She hadn't wanted to go to the market. She wanted to stay home. She wanted a lazy Saturday.

"I'm sorry," Peter says, tears welling in his eyes. "I didn't know. We wouldn't have gone if I knew." He wipes his nose on his protective gloves and glances back toward the night manager's office. He must see something because he adds, "Can we talk about this inside?"

Florence hates how reasonable he sounds. She wants him to beat his chest, pull out his hair. She's dying! "No! We can't talk about this inside! It's too late!" She means this literally. She'll be dead in days.

"Flo, please. We need to go—"

"What's going on over there?" The night manager yells. He's in the parking lot, and Florence can hear him coming toward them.

Florence forces herself to her feet and struggles up the embankment. Peter watches silently as she slips and slides in the muck. Eventually, she makes it to the top and retches in the grass. All that comes out is bile.

"You hear me?" The night manager hollers. "I don't want any trouble here." He's a short, bald man with a bushy goatee. As he approaches, he clicks on a long, black flashlight and points it at them. With the additional light, Florence can see he's wearing threadbare white gloves. The manager stops in the parking lot, twenty feet from the drainage ditch.

Peter is pale as milk. He forces a tight smile and wheels around to address the man. "We're good! Just an accident. You mind pointing your flashlight someplace else?" He's using his stage voice; the one that says *we're all having a great time*. Over his shoulder, he whispers to Florence, "Tell him you're fine."

Florence straightens. Nothing is fine. Everything has gone to hell. She wants to collapse into the grass and let the earth swallow her. None of this is fair. What did she do to deserve this?

"Flo, tell the man you're fine," Peter reiterates.

Florence waves at the night manager. Halfway through the gesture she realizes she's not wearing gloves and hides her hands behind her back. "Too much to drink. Thought it would be fun to play tag. Apparently, it's not." The lie rolls off her tongue so smoothly Florence isn't even sure how she came up with it.

"I'm not buying it," the night manager says. He flashes his light at her face, and she struggles not to block the beam with her bare hands. "I don't want trouble here. If you're causing trouble, you're gone. You understand? I don't need people coming and going at all hours of the night."

Peter steps in front of the beam. "Hey, pal, we get it. We're good. Sorry to disturb you. We'll go back to our room. You won't hear a peep from us."

Peter heads back to their room. He moves in a wide arc so as not to get close to the man. Florence waits a few heartbeats and follows. As she passes the night manager whispers, "Are you alright, ma'am? Did he hurt you?"

Florence feels the wail grow inside her again. She's very much not *alright*. She cups her mouth. When she sees the look of concern on the night manager's face, she nods her head to maintain the lie.

"I can help," the man says.

"No one can help me," Florence utters as tears wet her cheeks.

Back in their room, Peter starts to pack their belongings. Numbly, Florence moves past him and heads back to the bathroom. Instead of leaning against the pink tub, she sits on the edge and eyes Nancy's photo. It's still on the floor, where it fell when the pain came.

"Flo, we should leave," Peter calls to her from the main room. "Running around in the middle of the night isn't exactly keeping a low profile. He's going to remember our faces.

Two minutes later, Florence is in the back of the sedan and they're rolling through the night. She doesn't bother to ask where Peter is taking them. It doesn't matter.

"Do you want to talk?" Peter asks. He looks at Florence through the rearview mirror. His brown eyes are bloodshot, and his face is careworn. He's barely hanging on. Florence can only imagine how she looks. What she doesn't need to imagine is how she feels—she's half-drunk from exhaustion and stress.

"No," Florence says. What is there to say? She's terrified, angry, depressed. She's grieving for herself. And to complicate the situation, the emotions come in waves. And between the waves, there is numbness.

They're on an unmarked country road, the motel a few hours behind them. The sun has started its march across the sky to take another day from her. She hates it. It's silly, but a childish part of her had hoped the night would stretch forever and that she wouldn't have to confront a new day.

Out the car window, all she's seen is underbrush, brown fields, and beaten-down towns. Broken places filled with paranoia and mistrust of anyone who wasn't born there. In the early days of Solomon's, small towns and neighborhoods across the country set up isolated communities to protect themselves from the disease. Outsiders were killed for daring to enter these places. The first casualty was a young college student named Samuel Haywood who snuck into King Village, Texas to see his girlfriend. His death made headlines across the country, but no one was charged with his murder.

Today, there are thousands of these small communities across the country, all with their own laws. Most aren't completely shut off from the world, but they're dangerous places, especially after sundown.

Coming out of her sluggish mind, Florence stretches, arching her back so it cracks. She aches everywhere, but especially in the intangible places of her soul. She tracks back to earlier in the day when Peter said they needed a plan. He was right, she just couldn't handle creating one at that moment. Now, with so little time left, they need to act fast.

"Where are we?" She asks, a tinge of guilt in her voice for not knowing. She should be helping him. She knows she's leaning on him too hard. It's what she's always done.

"West Virginia."

"Where are we going?"

"Black Mountain."

Peter's friend Sam went there with his wife, Missy, at the start of the outbreak. Their reasoning, as far as Florence recalls, is that there are fewer people in rural and remote areas, which means fewer opportunities to catch the disease. Sam asked Peter and Florence to join him, but they didn't. Florence wanted to leave the city; Peter wanted to stay. Florence wishes she would have fought harder.

"We can't go there," Florence says. She can't believe Peter would even suggest it.

"There's nowhere else."

"I'm infected." It's the first time Florence has said the words out loud. If words can be heavy, these are two tons of granite. "The whole reason Sam and Missy left the city was to get away from people like me."

"I've known Sam for fourteen years. We can stay until you—"

"Until I die? That's what you were going to say, isn't it?"

They sit in silence. Florence fights back more tears. She never thought she could cry as hard as she did last night. The only time she came close was when Nancy died.

"Yes," Peter says five minutes later. He doesn't look her in the eye when he speaks, and it stings Florence more than his admission. "Sam will take us in. Just trust me on this, okay?"

Until I die. The words linger, running through her head on repeat, choking out everything around her. Opinions vary about what happens to the infected when they burst into light. Not everyone believes the infected die. A few months after the initial outbreak, there'd been a small but vocal movement of fanatics that believed Solomon's was a gateway to a new, better world. They called it The Gift and purposely infected themselves. For others, the disease is a way to transition to a higher state of consciousness where they can exist as pure thought.

Scientifically, there is no answer. It's a mystery that terrifies some and fascinates others. Florence believes that when the infected explode into motes of light and disappear, they die. Unlike Peter, however, she believes in an afterlife. She's unsure if there is a Heaven exactly, but her soul will live on.

They continue to sit in silence as the sun rises to midday. She can't believe she's spending the last days and hours of her life in a cramped, used car that reeks of stale sweat.

An hour later, Peter stops at an intersection and drums his hand on the steering wheel. "I think we're lost. How did people survive without phones?" He pulls a dingy road atlas from the glove box and examines it.

Florence gazes out the passenger side window. The grass along the side of the road is knee high and littered with yard signs advertising fresh eggs, firewood, and fruit. One sign reads *Fresh Meat Reasonably Priced.*

"I'm going to the bathroom," Florence says.

"Don't be long," Peter replies, and Florence rolls her eyes. What is she going to do? Run away?

Florence relieves herself in the tall grass. As she buttons her jeans, she studies the signs again. One stands out; it's smaller than the rest, with a gold glitter arrow pointing to the right. It reads: *Nancy's Birthday Party*. The sign is ancient and mostly faded. It could have been there for years.

Reading it makes Florence feel like she's been punched in the gut. Her Nancy's face fills her thoughts. How many birthdays did they spend together? Seven? Eight? Florence is angry and ashamed. *Why didn't you do anything?* She screams internally. *Because you're a coward!*

She's so fucking tired of it all, tired of being scared, tired of running from Nancy. In the far corners of her mind, she's always thought that one day she would find a way to make up for what she did.

"Time's running out," Florence says softly, and she realizes where she must go.

Peter has stepped out of the car and placed the atlas on the hood. His brow is scrunched together in concentration or frustration. Maybe both. Florence comes as close as she dares and swats at an errant black fly.

"We need to go that way," Peter says, motioning to the left. He snaps the atlas shut. "If we drive fast, we'll be there in a few hours. I'm positive Sam will let us stay. And if he doesn't, he'll at least give us some supplies."

"I don't want to go," Florence says quietly—so quietly, in fact, that she barely hears the words herself. Peter doesn't turn toward her and instead heads to the driver's side door. She clears her throat, tries again, only louder: "I don't want to go."

This time, Peter pays attention. He smooths his eyebrows with his thumb and forefinger. It's a habit Florence finds condescending. "We talked about this. You agreed."

"No. I told you they wouldn't take us in. You decided we were going anyway."

"It's a good plan."

"I don't want to go," Florence reiterates.

Peter crosses his arms and narrows his eyes. Somehow, it makes him look less imposing. "There's nowhere else." He gets into the car and motions for her to join him. When she doesn't follow, he rolls down the window. "Get in."

The ratty birthday sign seesaws in the breeze. It makes her feel closer to Nancy, as if she were drawing strength from her dead friend. "I want to go to Greenewin," she says. Florence lived in the town until Nancy died. Afterward, she and her family moved to Connecticut. Her mother used to say it was to be closer to her aging father, but Florence knows it was also because of what happened.

"Why? Nothing's there."

"Nancy's mother lives there."

"Your dead friend's mother lives there?" Peter blurts out. "No, that doesn't make sense. Do you even know her? It's a bad idea." He stiffens and Florence can sense that what he's about to say is difficult for him. "Do you really want to spend our last days together driving halfway across the country?"

Florence is hot all over. Peter always thinks he's right,

that he has the best ideas, that he knows what's good for them both. She likes this from time to time, even finds it attractive, but it can also be infuriating, especially when he doesn't take her seriously. She snorts and yanks open the back passenger door.

"Okay," Peter says, twisting to watch her. "I'm sorry, but this is the right decision."

Florence reaches into the car and jerks out her backpack. She slams the door and heads in the direction of the birthday party. How is she going to reach Greenewin? She doesn't know, but she must.

The car engine rumbles and Peter pulls beside her, matching her pace. Florence stops walking but doesn't face her boyfriend.

"Come on, what are you doing?" Peter asks.

"I'm going to Greenewin."

"Have you lost your *mind*?"

Florence spins on Peter, doing her best to keep calm. "I'm going to Greenewin," she says, through clenched teeth. "If you don't want to come with me, then leave. Go to Black Mountain. They'll take you in, as long as you aren't infected."

"Greenewin is…" Peter stammers. "I don't even know how far away it is, but you can't walk there. You won't make it."

"I'll hitchhike or steal a car. I'll figure it out."

"What's gotten into you?"

"I'm dying," Florence screams. She squeezes her eyes shut and tries to block out the world, but it does nothing. She screams again, and this time she clutches her hair with both hands. Folding into herself, she releases a powerful silent wail. Her entire body trembles and she shouts at Peter, "I'm dying, do you understand that? I don't have months or years! Everything has to be now! All of it!" She inhales and exhales through her nose, one, two, three times. She wants to stamp her feet and punch the world. She can't though. She can't let her anger steal what little time she has left. Especially now that she knows what she needs to do.

Straightening her bowed back, she looks Peter in the eye. To his credit, he doesn't look away, and he doesn't scold her for acting out. Maybe he's finally letting the truth sink in. He can't logic his way out of this situation. It doesn't matter how much planning they do, how much he wants to protect to her, how much he wants to be with her. This is the end.

"Peter, I know you don't understand, but I have to do this," Florence continues. "*I just have to.* I need to go to Greenewin. I want you to come with me, but I won't force you. But I'm going, with or without you. So, you need to make up your mind right now."

Peter doesn't speak. Florence doesn't know what he's going to do. She knows he loves her, but the disease has changed everything. If he were smart, and she knows he is, he'd leave her—take the car and go to Black Mountain on his own. The DPF would still be hunting him, but she wouldn't be slowing him down. She tells herself that it's okay if he leaves, that he needs to protect himself too. But Florence also knows it'll crush her.

After what feels like hours, Peter break eye contact

and glares down the road. "Get in," he says quietly, and Florence finally breathes. "You're probably right, anyway. Sam wouldn't take us in."

Chapter Five

Florence shudders awake with a gasp and moans in agony. She's feels like she's about to burst into flames. Soft yellow-orange light pulses from her skin. Biting her lower lip, she distracts herself by focusing on her surroundings. She's in the back seat of the car, parked in a field behind a dense row of trees and underbrush. It's daybreak and the air is heavy with the curious *coo* of a mourning dove. When the pain forces its way to the front of her mind once more, she concentrates on the rise and fall of her chest.

Just breathe, she thinks. *It's the easiest thing in the world.*

On her sixth breath, the world goes gray and the same peculiar pressure she felt when her right hand plunged into the bathroom tile envelops her body. She falls *through* the car door, and thumps into coarse crabgrass that jabs and pokes her soft spots. Curling into herself, she stares at her naked body. She might be turning incorporeal, but her clothes aren't.

This can't be happening, she thinks. Intellectually, she knows how the disease manifests, but experiencing it is surreal.

"Peter," she shrieks, "stay back!" Rising to her feet, Florence wobbles on shaky legs and steadies herself against the vehicle. A handful of tedious seconds pass, and when she thinks the worst of the pain is over, the arm she's using to balance herself drops through the car.

"Argh," Florence stammers, and yanks her hand out of the vehicle. She flicks her wrist back and forth as if she's trying to fling a viscous liquid from her fingers. As she works her hand, a new sensation comes over her, and her muscles tighten with anxiety. She feels light, as if she's somehow lost five pounds overnight. "I'm floating," she mutters, and sends a furtive glance down. What she sees sends shockwaves of panic through her. She's hovering like a partially deflated balloon. She barely has time to react before the invisible flames inside retreat into a dull ache and she plumets.

As a toddler, she begged her mother to let her fly like the bluejays in their backyard. She held onto this desire for years, and even as an adult she sometimes wished she could take to the air. This small, impractical, childish dream dies a swift bloody death in Florence's mind. She never again wants to fly. She wants to stay on the ground forever.

Florence stands frozen beside the car, glaring at her bare toes. She forces herself to take a gentle, testing step.

As her foot touches the grass, she collapses and grips the soil with both hands. *It's only going to get worse*, she thinks, and releases a silent scream at the suffering she must endure.

After a time, she sits up and wipes tears from the corner of her eyes and scans for Peter. He's nowhere in sight. She dresses and pulls her hair into a ponytail.

"Peter!" Florence calls and tenses when he doesn't reply.

"This isn't funny, Peter! Can you hear me?"

More nothing.

Stay calm. There are hundreds of reasons why Peter isn't here. He could be taking a piss. Maybe he heard something and is investigating.

She waits, the minutes piling up too fast for comfort. She wants to stay calm. But her fear forces her to panic. "Peter! Come back!" She screams at the top of her lungs and rushes around the edge of the field, hoping for any sign that he's nearby, footprints or broken underbrush.

Gradually, Florence realizes that she's alone, that Peter is gone. He left while she was sleeping. Her legs go weak, and she falls to her knees.

Florence never considered that Peter might leave her. She acted brave yesterday when she told him she'd find a way to Greenewin without him, but deep down, she knows it was an act. She's not that person—she's not brave.

When the outbreak started, Peter was the one who gathered supplies. And when Florence's mother died, Peter was the one who arranged the funeral. Without him,

Florence isn't sure she can reach Greenewin.

Tears stream down Florence's cheeks, and she wipes them away. "Get ahold of yourself," she says, fighting back the hysteria coursing through her veins. There has to be a reasonable and rational explanation. Think like Peter. Make a plan. Follow through.

She heads to the car, the last place he would have been, and is somewhat relieved when she finds his backpack and clothes are still there. But it's a brief balm because their money is missing.

Holding herself, Florence slumps against the car. There is nothing she can do but wait and trust Peter. Time crawls. Thirty minutes pass, then an hour. She relieves herself in the bushes and checks out the road they drove in on. When she gets bored enough, Florence traces Nancy's name into the dirt with a stick.

"What are you doing?" Peter asks as he pushes through the underbrush into the field. He carries a cardboard cup holder with two coffees in it in his right hand. A brown paper bag swings lazily from his left. His face is red, and his forehead is lathered with sweat.

Hearing his voice, Florence yelps with joy and rushes to him. Everything in her body tells her to throw herself into his arms. She wants Peter to wrap his strength around her. She wants him to stroke the back of her head and say everything will be all right. It takes an ungodly amount of willpower to stop herself. She skitters to a stop less than a foot from him and forces herself to take several steps back. "I thought you left me."

Peter's face twists like he's been stabbed, and Florence

immediately regrets her words. Just look at everything he's done already. Peter doesn't have to be here. He could have left her on the highway and headed off to Black Mountain to join Sam and Missy.

"I'm sorry," Florence says and drops her eyes. "I…I panicked. I was scared." She chuckles and wraps her arms around her stomach. It's not funny, but she doesn't know what else to do.

"It's okay," he says, but Florence can tell she hurt him.

Florence wipes a tear from her face. She feels like that is all she's done in the last two-and-a-half days, cry and cry and cry.

"Where did you go?" she asks, and the tension in the air fades away. Peter's intensity dissolves, and he returns to normal.

"Provisions." He jingles the brown bag in front of her. "I bought canned goods and water. Matches and other paraphernalia." He digs into the bag and pulls out two baseball caps. They're tan with a logo she doesn't recognize. He tugs on his hat and adds a pair of large black sunglasses. "How do I look?"

"Like you're about to catch the world's biggest bluegill."

"Perfect." He sets the other hat and a pair of sunglasses in front of her. "Now, we're ready to blend in."

Florence sniffles and tries on the hat and glasses. She feels ridiculous.

"Will you model it for me?"

"I certainly will not. This isn't Milan."

Peter raises an eyebrow and Florence decides to humor him. She strolls away from him through the grass with exaggerated hip swings. After a few strides, she spins, and points one hand to the sky. She has no idea where the pose came from.

Peter catcalls. "Very nice. You're very stylish in your ugly hat and dirty clothes."

Florence bows and instantly feels better. He always knows how to make her smile, even when she doesn't know how to do it herself.

"Alright, Gigi Hadid, come and get your breakfast— that is, if you're eating today."

Florence has no appetite, but she knows she must eat. Peter places a cup of coffee on the ground and adds a massive chocolate muffin, her favorite. Peter bought banana bread and an apple for himself. They pick at their food in silence.

"Flo," Peter says after a time, "I know this is all my fault. I asked you to come with me when you didn't want to. I didn't infect you, but I put the wheels in motion. I know it, and I'm going to spend the rest of my life regretting it. I promise you, whatever happens, I'm not going to leave you. I'll carry you to Greenewin on my back if I have to. These moments are all we have left. I refuse to give them up. We've been through too much together for me not to be there in the end." As he finishes, he looks up from his breakfast. His face is drawn and sagging. He's powering through on will alone and trying not to show it.

Florence hasn't seen him like this since early in the outbreak when he was spiraling into a deep depression and sleeping only a few hours a night. She'd coaxed him out of his hopelessness with weeks of encouragement and by constructing a "movie theatre" on their roof, using a low-quality projector and white bedspread. She remembers climbing up the fire escape for the first time to reach her roof and how she gripped the ladder rungs so tight her fingers throbbed.

Florence blinks away more tears. She loves him and is scared for him. Peter would grind himself into dust for her. His father died from a stroke before the outbreak. He doesn't even know his mother's name. If he has cousins, they are so distant they might as well be strangers. She's all he has in the world. She's his family.

"I want you with me until the end," she says tentatively. "I don't want to do this alone, but you need to promise me—swear to me—that you won't put yourself in danger. If I can't live the life I wanted, I need you to do it for me. Do you understand?"

"I won't leave you," Peter says.

"Promise me. You need to stay alive."

"I should have done this a long time ago," Peter says, ignoring her plea. He stands and digs in his pocket. When he finds what he's looking for, he keeps it hidden in his closed fist.

Florence knows what's coming, but wishes it wasn't. It's only going to make things more difficult. Peter opens his hand. Laying on his palm is a semi-transparent orange ring with a chunky rectangular top. "Will you marry me?"

Florence clutches her heart, not because she doesn't love Peter, but because she's scared he'll try to put the ring on her finger.

A long pause follows. As he waits for her to answer, his bottom lip starts to quiver. It's obvious he expected an enthusiastic yes. "It's not what I wanted to give you," Peter blurts out, "but it's what I have. It's one-of-a-kind. A local artist was selling her jewelry at the coffee shop."

Florence throws up her hands and Peter stop talking. "Peter, I love you, but you must promise me. I can't say yes unless you promise me."

"I can't."

"You must. I mean it."

Dropping his arm, Peter studies the resin ring, then clenches his fist around it. "I thought we had more time, a future, a family. I would have made a good father."

You still can, Florence thinks. *You will.* "Peter, I need you to say it."

He opens his fist again and gently sets the ring in the grass. He steps away, giving Florence space to take it. He sniffles and rubs his eyes. "I promise."

Can I believe him? Florence asks herself. She wants to, needs to. "Yes," she says. "Always, yes."

She jets to the ring. It's large, but barely weighs any-thing. She slides the ring on over her gloved finger, and crooks her finger to keep it from falling off. "It's perfect."

Chapter Six

"We need gas," Peter says.

Up ahead is a grimy gas station that looks like it's held together by rust and water stains. The large yellow and blue sign that should be mounted high on a pole in front of the store is propped up in the bed of an old, broken down utility trailer parked near the entrance. Squat and square, the station looks like it was a mom-and-pop store years ago. A canopy covers two pumps, one of which is blocked by an imposing black pickup truck. As they approach, Florence frowns. Neither the gas station nor the truck looks friendly.

"We should go someplace else," Florence says.

"We're running on fumes," Peter replies, "and we don't know when we'll come across another station. It's now or never."

Florence leans back in her seat, unhappy with the

situation, but not sure how to change it. Peter is right. They've been on the road since noon, and they haven't seen an in-service station. It's what happens when there's a labor shortage and you avoid highways.

Peter eases into the station and parks behind the truck. He cuts the engine and pulls their cash from the glove compartment and counts it. As he flips through the bills, Florence peers at the pickup. A red sticker with the phrase "Gun Control Means Using Both Hands" is stuck to the left side of the bumper. On the right is a second sticker that reads, "I'd Rather Be Hunting."

Pushing the stickers out of her mind is impossible, no matter how hard she tries. Guns make her queasy. After the initial outbreak, gun deaths in America escalated swiftly. Everyone was scared and paranoid. It was as if the nation's empathy had dissolved in days. Carol, an acquaintance of Florence's from college was shot in the neck and killed when her puppy escaped and she chased the mutt into an elderly couple's lawn.

Florence and Peter had their own brush with a paranoid gun owner too. Though, thankfully, they escaped without a scratch. On occasion, when it was late and dark and the sidewalks and roads were empty, the two of them would take walks at the local park. It was little more than an oval track surrounding an abandoned soccer field, but it was a luxury she knew not everyone had.

It was a Wednesday, close to 11 p.m. though she can't remember the exact time. They were walking the track in silence because they'd exhausted everything they could possibly talk about having been in lockdown for months.

A man in all black emerged from the shadows ahead of them, and before either of them could react, he pulled a handgun and shouted for them to back away.

Peter instinctually stepped in front Florence and told the man that they didn't have any money. He thought the man was trying to rob them, something that was common in those days, with so many people out of work and the cost of food soring.

"I don't want your fucking money," the man snarled. "Get out of my way!" He jabbed the gun at them and directed them to the soccer field.

"What the hell is wrong with you?" Peter shouted back.

Florence was certain the man was going to kill them. It happened all the time. The world isn't as it once was; or maybe it never was in the first place.

The man told them that if they didn't get off the track and lay down in the field, they wouldn't see dawn. Peter backed the pair of them into the field with Florence pressed to his back. When they were far enough away, Peter whispered that if the man fired, Florence should run. He'd rush the guy as a distraction.

It wasn't necessary. The man in black backpedaled down the track and disappeared into the night. It was the last time they walked the track.

"Charming clientele," Florence says, peeling her eyes off the bumper sticker.

Peter ignores her comment. "Do you want anything? Soda? Zebra Cake?"

Florence shakes her head. "No, I'm okay."

A red arrow points to restrooms at the side of the structure. Seeing the signs makes Florence's skin itch. In the last couple of days, she's sweated through her clothes more than once. She craves a hot shower with steam so thick she could cut it with knife.

"I'm going to clean up," she says, removing her engagement ring and dropping it into the cupholder. She doesn't want to walk around with it loose on her finger.

Peter gives her a tight, worried smile. "Be careful."

"If anyone's there, I'll come back."

Florence shoulders her backpack and pads to the restrooms. Her path takes her past the station's front window. Inside, an old man with a thick white beard and a dingy ball cap that might once have been light gray eyes her from the customer side of the counter. A middle-aged woman in a red vest opposite the man does the same. The attention shoots a spike of adrenaline through Florence. She lowers her chin and looks slightly to the right so they can't get a good look at her. Adding a police chase to their trip would be a terrible idea.

She knocks loudly on the bathroom door three times, and when no one answers, she pushes inside. She expects a rush of putrid air, sophomoric graffiti, and doorless stalls. She couldn't have been more wrong. The restroom is bright white and immaculately clean. The faint smell of lemons lingers. "Hello, anyone in here?"

Two pale blue stalls are in the restroom, along with two sinks. She carefully inches inside the room just in case some else is inside. Peeking into both stalls, she relaxes. She's alone. A few minutes away from the car to stretch and recharge is an extravagance. She locks the door to be safe and heads to the first sink.

The water that comes out of the tap is hot but not scalding. It feels good on her skin, refreshing. She plugs the sinks with brown paper towels and lets the water run. As the basin fills, she studies herself in the mirror above the sink. After removing the hat Peter bought her, she runs her fingers through her greasy hair. She forgot her comb at the apartment. Thankfully, she hasn't broken out from stress, but she can feel pimples pressing at the underside of her skin.

"You look like shit," Florence says to her reflection and makes a note to tell Peter to use the best picture he has of her at her funeral—the one from when they went to Brighton Beach, and she wore that big floppy hat. Her mother's funeral was intimate and powerful. Close friends and family placed items that reminded them of her mother in a remembrance casket, a shoebox sized wooden container that's buried in lieu of a body. It was a touching service. She wants the same.

Florence turns off the faucet, removes her gloves, and plunges her arms into the water. It's warm and soothing, just like she wanted. She splashes her forearms and uses two generous squirts of neon pink soap to scrub away the built-up grime. The clear water in the basin instantly turns filthy gray, and, disgusted with herself, she drains the sink and refills it.

Five minutes later, she shakes the excess water from her body and pats herself dry with paper towels. The spare shirt she packed is a long sleeve black number with holes in the cuffs to slip her thumbs through. Years ago, it belonged to Peter. He "bequeathed" it to her on her thirtieth birthday. Though threadbare, it fits her perfectly. Oversized and loose, it hangs from her shoulder and sways when she walks. She should have worn the shirt from the start. Wearing it is like wrapping herself in Peter's strength and love. She tucks the shirt into her jeans to stop the remote possibility of a breeze exposing her stomach and lower back. After, she brushes her teeth and runs her fingers through her oily hair.

Better, she thinks, examining herself in the mirror again. *More human than feral animal.* She feels good enough to let herself believe she'll reach Greenewin before she dies. Her pleasant mood crashes with an intrusive thought. *What will she say to Nancy's mother?* She knows she needs to figure it out, but she doesn't have the perfect words. She doesn't even have imperfect words. Twenty years—that's how long she's had to uncover the right words to make it all make sense, and she still hasn't come close. Now she has forty-eight hours, maybe less, to get the words right. *Impossible.*

Florence's backpack stands agape on the floor. She pulls out her diary and flips through it until she finds Nancy's picture. Still annoyed about the dogeared corner, she tries again to smooth the fold with her thumb and pointer finger. Like before, she can't fix it.

"What's going to happen to you when I'm gone?" Florence asks the picture. Nancy's mother took the photo with an old camera Florence found in a junk drawer. Florence developed it a week later and wedged it into the corner of a corkboard in her bedroom. She's positive Nancy's mother has never seen it. *She should have it,* Florence thinks. The photo is a little piece of Nancy. It belongs with Mrs. Barnes, not buried in a remembrance casket.

Flipping it over, Florence studies the back of the photo. It's blank. If someone found it in fifty years, they wouldn't know who was in the photo. She unzips the small pocket on the front of her bag and digs around until she finds a black pen and in the bottom left corner writes the year the picture was taken, and Nancy and her names. Then inspiration strikes and Florence scribbles a short letter to Mrs. Barnes and makes a mental note to tell Peter to give the picture to Nancy's mother if she doesn't make it to Greenewin.

> *Mrs. Barnes,*
> *I want you to have this. I'm sorry for what I did.*
> *Florence*

In the bottom right, she adds the date. Then, as a precaution:

> *If found, mail to Kathleen Barnes.*
> *1347 Tumner Lane*
> *Greenewin, MN 49068*

Florence examines both sides of the photo a couple more times, returns it to her notebook, packs her belongings, and heads back to the car.

Turning the building's corner, she sees Peter leaning

against the hood, sipping cheap coffee from a large Styrofoam cup. A second coffee rests on the roof of the vehicle. "I got us some more go-juice and a couple of waters."

The bearded man in the dirty gray cap that Florence noticed on her way to the restroom emerges from the store. He's older than she initially thought, somewhere in his early sixties. A thick olive jacket flaps around his slight paunch. Camouflage gloves protect his hands. He takes an exaggerated arc around the two of them as he humps to his truck. He looked unfriendly when Florence passed him earlier, more so now. Florence's heart speeds up. People are paranoid for a reason, she reminds herself. When you live in a world where accidentally brushing against someone could mean death, you adapt. As long as they don't rush the man, Florence reminds herself, they'll be safe.

Florence drops her chin again and turns her face away from the man. Then she chides herself for her trip to the restroom. She should have had Peter buy a gallon of water and a bar of soap. As inconvenient as it might be, bathing in an alley or in the woods would be safer. No one would recognize her then. Every local station runs DPF-provided photos of notable runners three times a day. Descriptions of runners are also shared over the radio. There was a time when Florence watched the evening updates, hoping not to see a friend's headshot pop up. Peter made her stop. It was making them both crazy.

"Hey," the old, bearded man shouts from the passenger side of the truck.

Florence startles and tries hard to hide it. *Get to the*

car and get out of this place, she thinks. *Why didn't we concoct a backstory?* Someone was going to ask questions. Humans always do.

"Yeah?" Peter answers as he turns to face the man.

"Passing through or staying?"

"Why do you ask?"

"This ain't a hospitable place to strangers."

"What place is?"

"Fair enough. Just be out of here by sundown. The town closes at night. No one in. No one out."

"Thanks for the advice."

The old man shakes his head and huffs. "Ain't advice. It's a warning."

Peter bristles and his face flushes, a telltale sign that he's pissed. Florence knows him well enough that it's a near certainty that he's going to make a snide remark, like ask the man if his large truck is compensating for his insecurities. It can't happen. She won't let it happen. They need to be smarter.

"You ready to go?" Florence calls. She's halfway to Peter, in the open space between their car and the entrance to the gas station.

Peter peels his eyes from the man to focus on her. "Yeah, all gassed up?"

A soft swooshing to Florence's right draws her attention. The woman in the red vest exits the main building. "What the actual fuck is going on here, James?" she shouts. "I told you to leave these people alone. We don't need you scaring away customers." She addresses Florence and Peter. "You ignore him. He's just an old man who can't find anything better to do than harass people."

"Town closes at sundown, Heather," he barks back.

"What are you going to do? Shoot everyone who passes through?"

"Someone has to protect this place."

"It doesn't have to be you."

"We'll be on our way," Florence calls out.

She makes it three steps before she realizes she's glowing yellow-orange. *Please, not now,* she thinks. Her body doesn't listen. An inferno rages through her nerves, and she calls out in shock and agony. Her pack and clothes tumble through her and land in a sloppy pile. Through the fire that is her flesh, she thinks: *Solomon's is stealing my body!* Weightlessness follows. She grimaces and maneuvers her torso back and forth to keep her balance and stop herself from tipping over.

The old man shouts incoherently and lunges at the passenger door of his truck. Out of the corner of her eye, Florence sees Heather dart inside the gas station. In front of her, Peter drops his Styrofoam cup, splashing coffee over his shoes. In an instant, he goes from a standstill to striding toward her, worry written across his face. This is the first time he's witnessed her symptoms, seen the disease try to pull her apart.

"Don't come any closer," she rasps through the pain. Starting with her toes, she concentrates on each body part and tells herself she's still alive, still on Earth, still whole. As quickly as the symptoms came on, they stop, and her stomach settles into itself. She drops back to the ground and bends over. Sweat spills from her brow, darkening the blacktop. It's become more difficult to fight the symptoms. It's as if her body *wants* to break apart and disappear.

"God damn runner," James growls.

Looking up from the ground, Florence freezes, stunned by what she sees. The old man glares at her through the scope of a black hunting rifle. She has time to realize his hands are shaking before he fires. A loud bang thunders through the air. Florence flinches and instinctively shrinks into herself. She's certain the old man has blasted a hole in her chest the size of Manhattan. But James hasn't shot her. He missed, and now his face is contorted in confusion.

Roaring, Peter rushes James, head down, arms spread. He barrels into the old man, and they tumble to the ground in a heap and grapple for the rifle. The sickening sound of fists on soft flesh makes Florence gag. James clubs Peter's face over and over. He might be old, but the bearded man isn't weak.

Florence feels like a mountain again, incapable of moving, incapable of saving Peter. Long horrifying seconds pass, and still, she doesn't react. *This is how you killed Nancy! Not again!* She forces her legs to move. As she reaches them, another shot rings out, and Peter slumps off James, clutching his left shoulder. Vibrant red blood leaks through his fingers, and his face twists in a combination of surprise and pain.

"You shot him!" Florence says her voice cracking. The world goes still and silent. Anger takes hold of her. How dare this insignificant man take Peter from her? "You monster!"

James sits up and points the rifle at Peter. The muzzle bounces erratically from his trembling hands. He huffs, and to Florence's surprise, he doesn't pull the trigger. Instead, he pushes away from Peter with his legs and backs into his truck. The righteousness that ruled him is gone.

A deep moan draws Florence's attention. Peter is on his back, grimacing, both hands clinging to an expanding red spot on his shirt. They lock eyes. Florence did this. She didn't mean to, but she made it happen. "Go," Peter stammers.

She can't run, not when Peter needs her. She screams at the top of her lungs and charges the old man. What she wants is to grab him and wrap her naked body against him. She wants to give James what he most fears. "I'm going to infect you!"

The old man mouths a jumble of syllables. He tries to point his rifle at Florence but the weapon slips from his hands and slaps the blacktop. He throws his hands in front of his face. "I have a wife! I have grandbabies!"

She slows at the last moment. The hate is still there. It will never go away. Still, she can bury it. She won't be what this man thinks she is. Her hands quiver as she grabs the hunting rifle and aims it at the man. She has no idea how to use it. She doesn't even know if it's loaded. "Get up and run! Or so help me, I'll put a bullet in you!"

James gives her a helpless look before lumbering to his feet. He doesn't run fast.

"Flo, the clerk," Peter says. He directs her attention to Heather. She's screaming at them from the gas station's front door, smartphone in hand.

"I called the DPF! They're coming for you!" She backs into the store and locks the sliding glass door.

"We have to go," Peter hisses through clinched teeth.

Florence tosses the rifle to the side and tries to help Peter to his feet, but as she approaches, he waves her off. "Stop," he barks. "You can't touch me."

Fuck, Florence silently screams.

With a painfully loud grunt, Peter plants one foot on the ground and forces himself to stand. He stumbles to the car, blood trailing every step and leans against the door. Wincing, he digs into his pocket and tosses Florence the keys to the vehicle. They're warm and slick with gore. She swallows the fear in her throat and barely manages not to drop the keys.

"You're in the driver's seat now," he says.

Chapter Seven

"This is going to hurt," Florence says as she sets a brown bottle of peroxide and four rolls of gauze on the ground in front of Peter. He leans bare-chested against the passenger side of the car, one hand pressing his black shirt against his wound to stem the bleeding. Florence steps back and tugs up her protective gloves. She's in Peter's spare set of clothes, black jeans rolled up several times, a thin, billowing white hoodie, black socks, and a cheap pair of sandals she'd forgotten were in the trunk.

Peter snatches up the bottle, twists off the cap with his teeth, and splashes the clear liquid on the bloody injury. He hisses and squeezes his eyes shut as the peroxide fizzes and bubbles. When the sound dies down, he awkwardly wraps the wound and leans on the car again. Beads of sweat race down his bruised and lacerated face and drip off his chin. "Just like Rambo," he murmurs.

The two of them are in the gravel parking lot of an abandoned factory, ninety minutes from the gas station.

"Are you okay?" Florence asks. It's a dumb question but she doesn't know what else to say. She can't help him bandage his wound or comfort him with a gentle touch. *Together, we are islands,* she thinks. She's never felt this way before, and it racks her heart.

Peter breathes in and out slowly. "I'm fine," he says, but it's clear he's lying. He flings his shaggy hair out of his eyes and shoots her a crooked smile. It's what made her fall in love with him when they met for coffee all those years ago. He's a good-looking man. Kind, too. Before the outbreak he volunteered at the community center, helping teens learn to play the guitar.

"You're not fine," Florence protests. It's just like him to play it cool. While he might be kind, he's also stubborn. "You were nearly killed. You were literally shot."

"'Tis but a scratch," Peter says, quoting *Monty Python and the Holy Grail*, a film he makes her watch at least twice a year.

This is supposed to make Florence feel better, to calm her down and imply that everything is hunky-dory or some other twee saying. It does the opposite. Frustration flares through her. "Don't joke about this. This isn't a game."

Peter blanches, clearly not expecting such a strong response. "I'm sorry. It hurts. Quite a lot actually and I was positive that was the end of me. No more tomorrow. No more anything."

Florence sympathizes. Her mind is thick with

thoughts of her own mortality.

"Is this what it's like?" Peter asks. Instead of looking at her, he stares at the bloody shirt in the gravel and pokes it with his shoe.

"Every second," Florence replies.

"I'm sorry."

"So am I."

Peter sniffs. "Do we have any Advil?"

"I have a bottle in my bag." Florence walks to the driver's side of the car and searches the back seat for her backpack. Her heart rate increases a little when she doesn't find it immediately, then it rockets to the moon when she realizes it's not where it should be.

"Have you seen my bag?" she asks, pushing down the worry building inside her. It makes no sense why Peter would have it, but she needs to know.

"You had it with you at the gas station."

Bile rises in the back of Florence's throat. She throws herself into the car. It's not there. If it was, she would have found it already. There is no place for it to hide. A beat passes. "It's not in the car," she says, rising to meet Peter's gaze. They stare at each other over the hood of the car. "I dropped it at the gas station."

"It's okay," Peter says. "We can buy more Advil and clothes."

"It's not *okay*." The ferocity in Florence's voice scares her and she checks herself. In a lower register, she adds, "My notebook was in there. *Nancy's picture was in it*."

"Flo, it's a *picture*," Peter replies. "We have bigger things to worry about—I was shot!"

"You don't understand," Florence answers. "It's not *just a picture*. I wrote Mrs. Barnes' address on the back."

"Shit," Peter utters and slams the car door shut. He limps away and runs his bloody fingers through his hair, gathering his thoughts. After what feels like an eternity, Peter looks back at Florence and she deflates. She knows what he's going to say before he says it. "We can't go there anymore, Flo. I know you want to, but we can't. The DPF will be there."

Florence bites her tongue to keep from wailing. She doesn't *want* to go to Greenewin—she *needs* to go to Greenewin. But Peter has a point; she can't deny it. It's more dangerous than before. If they go, they might both get themselves killed. Which isn't much to Florence. She's dead either way. But Peter…she won't have his death on her conscience.

Florence studies Peter's body. She knows it like her own. She loves that his beard hair is slightly darker than the rest of the hair on his body. She's traced the stretch marks on his stomach a thousand times. His fingertips are calloused from his guitar. Florence loves this man, and he's done everything in his power to keep her alive so far. To keep both of them alive.

Peter waits for Florence to speak. When she doesn't, he says, "You don't have to do this. Whatever happened back then doesn't matter. We can go away together. We can enjoy the time we have left. Flo, please, I love you."

Florence doesn't know how to respond. Her mind plays out the fantasy. They would find some place nearby. There would be bonfires at night. He'd find a guitar somehow and sing "One Hundred Ways to Love You," a song he wrote for her on their first anniversary. The song is cheesy and sweet and perfect. She can hear the lyrics in her mind. *I know one hundred ways to love you. Tomorrow I'll learn one hundred more.*

She also hears Nancy's voice calling to her. She's heard it again and again for years on top of years. It haunts her. She can't die without making things right with Mrs. Barnes; she can't die with that weight.

There is one thing she can do, Florence knows. But she needs to find the strength. She needs to be brave for Peter and herself.

"Are you going to say anything, Flo?" Peter asks.

"You're right. We can't go to Greenewin. Not if they know we're coming."

Peter stiffens from shock. By the look on his face, he expected a fight. "I'm sorry. I know how important this is to you."

Florence shuts the driver's side rear door and sits down behind the steering wheel. She jams the keys into the ignition and locks herself inside. Her stomach roils with anxiety.

"What are you doing?" Peter mouths, rapidly slapping the car in panic.

Florence cracks the passenger side window enough that they can hear each other. "Go to Black Mountain. If I'm not with you, Sam and Missy will let you in."

"Stop," Peter says. "Turn the car off."

"I can't. And you know I can't. I have to do this alone."

Peter stops pounding. His voice goes weak. "I'll go with you, Flo. If it means that much to you, I'll go with you. I don't want this to be the end. I don't want this to be how I remember you."

That does it. Tears flow freely down Florence's cheeks.

Peter edges around until he's outside the driver's side window. "I'll go with you," he reiterates.

"If you come with me, you're going to get yourself killed." She takes a deep, deep breath, one that touches her soul. When she's as calm as she's going to be, Florence pulls their money from the glove compartment and takes a few bills. She lowers the driver's side window an inch and pushes the rest of the cash through the opening. It should be enough to get Peter to Black Mountain. He'll need to be smart and lucky, but Florence believes in him.

To drive the point home, she fumbles for her engagement ring in the cupholder. She's never lifted something so heavy. She slips it on her ring finger over her glove and kisses its crown. She imagines what their future could have looked like, and then she takes it off and pushes it through the window opening.

Peter stares at it in disbelief. He blinks hard and his posture shifts. His shoulders sag, and Florence knows he's resigned to reality. He knows he can't stop her. "I don't understand," he says quietly. As he does, he pulls the glove from his right hand and presses it to the window. "But I believe in you."

Florence blinks back more tears, pulls off her own glove, and moves to press her palm against the inside of the window. Her body yearns for Peter. She wants to feel his warmth more than she ever has before. She wants to feel his arms wrap around her shoulders, his breath on her neck. But this is the closest they will ever come to being with each other again.

As she moves her hand toward the glass, Florence sees Peter's blood-tinted hands. *You did that! It's your fault!* Florence pauses, her own hand close but not touching the glass. She must be strong. It's too dangerous to touch the glass, not with Peter so close. She knows what could happen. The scene flashes before her eyes. She sees the disease torturing her body. She sees her hand pierce through the fragile window. She sees herself touching Peter, infecting him, killing him with her own carelessness. *It's my turn to protect him.*

"I love you," she whispers as she pulls her hand back. Then she drives away.

Chapter Eight

Twenty Years Ago

"I need a deep wish," Florence says as she wipes tears from her eyes. She's been crying for an hour and is exhausted. "I'll feel better after."

Three summers ago, the two of them invented the ritual. When they wanted something bad enough, they'd whisper their wish into a small rock and sink it in the lake. The greater the wish, the deeper the water.

Sitting on the dock beside Florence, Nancy kicks absently at the lake water. Instead of answering, she twists around to stare at the incoming storm. Florence does the same. Bulbous dark gray clouds are devouring the late afternoon daylight. In an hour or two, the clouds will reach French Lake and release a downpour strong enough to soak a walleye. That's what Channel 10's weatherman said, anyway.

"I don't know, Flo," Nancy says after a while and returns to kicking the lake. "It's going to rain."

Florence deflates. Nancy is right. They don't want to be on the lake when the storm hits. Especially not in Nancy's crappy little canoe. As much as they love it, the boat is leaky and unstable. It's also a pain in the butt to steer. Still, Florence asks Nancy for so little. If they move fast, like right this very second, Florence is positive she can make a deep wish before the storm hits—and then everything will be better. Or at least tolerable. She'll settle for tolerable.

Wordlessly, Nancy scoots across the dock, wraps an arm around Florence, and pulls her close. Florence's world fills with Nancy's pleasant scent, vanilla lotion, and sweat. More tears well in Florence's eyes, and she blinks them away as best she can. She's so tired of crying. She hates her body for making her do it.

"Joshua is an asshole," Nancy says. "You deserve better. A lot better."

"He's the Mayor Asshole of Asshole Land," Florence replies. It feels good to get it out. She's not usually this mean—but some people deserve it.

"He's the Once and Future King of Douche-dom," Nancy adds.

Florence giggles. It feels good to smile again. Her tired brain trips over itself for another insult worthy of Joshua Steddler. All she can think about are the cheesy space shows her father watches. "He's the Supreme Emperor of the Galactic Federation of Shitheads."

Nancy snorts and covers her mouth to kill the sound. Florence giggles in response. Nancy hates that she snorts, but Florence likes it. It makes Nancy seem normal. "May his reign be short," Nancy says in a mock chant and nuzzles into Florence's shoulder.

This is nice, Florence thinks. Nancy has every right tell her I told you so, but she won't. That's why they're friends. Reason one-thousand-and-nineteen of a million. Try as she might, though, Florence's idiot brain won't stop replaying the day. It's maddening.

When you go to a small school, you get to know your classmates well. Joshua is a good athlete. Loves basketball but is better at baseball. Every summer, he spends a week in Cincinnati with his grandparents. He says it's boring but talks about it all the time.

He's also stupidly handsome. Everyone agrees. Even Nancy, though she hates to acknowledge it. He has curly hair that bobs up and down over his eyes when he runs. His shoulders are broad and muscular, and his legs are thick and strong but not tree trunks. He dresses nice, and he smells good even after gym class.

On Saturday, Joshua asked her to see a movie with him, and Florence thought it was a joke because Nancy was the only person who asked her to do anything. But it wasn't a joke, and that afternoon they went to Fields County Mall to see a movie about two detectives who have to save a governor's daughter from…something. Florence can't remember because when the movie started, Joshua put his left hand on her thigh and kept it there for the entire show, sliding it slowly higher, one eyelash at a time. His touch made her feel like she had swallowed a volcano.

By the time they left the theater, she was floating.

She floated through a walk around the mall. She floated through an early dinner at Big Sam's Ultimate Slice. She floated through the twenty-minute bus ride to Adam's Park.

When Joshua finally kissed her, Florence knew she was never coming down. She went up on her toes to meet his lips. He tasted salty and hot. *I CAN'T BELIEVE THIS IS HAPPENING!* ran on repeat through her dizzy brain.

Then Monday happened.

Today happened.

Four hours ago happened.

Joshua told Blake Williams, who everyone knows can't keep a secret, that Florence kisses like a slobbering dog. Blake told Stacy Wall, and by lunch, everyone in the school knew what Joshua had said. That's bad enough, but then Stan Clay, who has a thin little mustache and smells like he doesn't shower, barked at her in the hall as they were changing classes, and everyone joined in.

Even Joshua.

Now Florence is here on this dock, and all she wants is to feel better. And she can make that happen; she can make a deep wish.

"Nancy," she says slowly, "I really need this."

Nancy pulls away. "You can make a wish from here. This is a good spot. The water is deep."

"It's not deep enough. It doesn't have…" Florence searches for the right words, "…the same magic. I want this wish to actually come true."

"Can't we watch a movie instead? My mom left us

money for pizza. We can do it in the morning before school."

It's a good idea. If Florence was smart, she'd listen to Nancy. But Florence doesn't want to be practical. "I want to do it tonight."

"Why are you in such a hurry?" Nancy snaps. Her voice is loud and strong. The athlete in her is showing. The competitor. "Why today?"

Good question. Florence dips a toe into the lake. It's cold for this time of the year, not that French Lake is ever warm. "You wouldn't understand."

"If you want me to go with you, make me understand." Nancy pulls her legs out of the water and readjusts to face Florence's side. "Look, I'm sorry. I didn't mean to snap at you. But you aren't acting like yourself. You don't even like making wishes, and now it's the most important thing in the world to you."

"Nancy, sometimes when I'm with you, I feel like no one notices me. You're...." She struggles, chokes back her words, afraid she'll hurt her friend. It's the last thing she wants to do.

"I'm what?"

"I don't want to."

"If I'm hurting you, I want you to tell me. You're my best friend."

"You're my best friend too. You aren't doing anything on purpose. But you're beautiful and popular and smart. And I'm me. And sometimes, when we're together, I don't think people see me. Not the way they see you." She's felt this way for a long, long time. "I thought Joshua actually liked me. I wish he hadn't asked me out. At least I wouldn't have gotten excited."

Nancy's face drops, and she looks away. "I'm sorry."

"It's not you," Florence sputters quickly. "You didn't do anything wrong. I just wish someone I liked would like me back. I want to feel special too."

"You are special."

"You know what I mean."

Nancy nods but doesn't reply.

"I'm tired of waiting," Florence says. "That's why it has to be today."

Nancy doesn't answer. Instead, she glances over her shoulder at the storm. Her face is unreadable. The frustrated knot in Florence's stomach expands until her whole body is tight. She desperately wants to make a deep wish. But she can't do it alone. She's not strong enough. Her arms would fall off before she was halfway there. She needs Nancy—and Nancy knows it.

"Okay, I'll help," Nancy says carefully, and the tension in Florence's body releases. "But you have to promise me something."

"Anything."

"We'll do it quickly."

"As fast as jackrabbits."

Nancy rises to her feet and pulls Florence up after. She looks her in the eye. "There's something else. Promise me you won't freeze."

Nancy knows her so well. Sometimes when she's surprised or scared, Florence turns into a statue. She's there in the canoe but also outside herself at the same time.

It's a big ask because it isn't like Florence can one-hundred-percent control what her body does. But if there was ever a time when she could do it, it'd be now.

"I promise," Florence says. She makes an X over her heart with her pinky, kisses it, and holds her finger out to Florence. "Until the stars fall," she adds. It's their promise, the one they use when they mean every word. To break the promise is unthinkable. It's the foundation of everything. It's their strength.

"Until the stars fall," Nancy replies. She makes the same motion and then wraps her pinky around Florence's. They hug and, after a time, Nancy races down the dock and across the shoreline to the overturned canoe.

Florence follows close behind but stops at a wooden storage chest at the end of the dock. Inside, buried under inflatable water toys and kickboards, is a rusty coffee tin filled with small rocks Florence and Nancy collected. She shakes the can a few times and digs around until she finds a smooth oblong rock the color of cream. Its surface is striped with thin white wavy lines. *Beautiful*, Florence thinks as she plucks the rock from the can. She jogs to Nancy and holds it out to show her friend.

"It's perfect," Nancy says. The canoe is half in the lake, and Nancy is bent over, holding it steady. "Grab the paddles and climb in."

♦♦♦

From above, French Lake looks like a malformed crab with arms protruding from the northwest and southwest ends of the lake. Nancy's home is situated on the southwestern crab arm, with the main body of water to the right. To the left, the crab arm tapers into a cove. On a calm day, Florence and Nancy can reach the middle of the lake in about forty minutes. They can reach the cove in twenty.

"Hold on," Nancy says. The canoe sways wildly as Nancy launches the craft into the lake. Seated at the front of the canoe, Florence grips the boat's sides tightly as it rocks back and forth. Nancy sloshes through the shallow water to her knees and bounds into the canoe, nearly capsizing it.

"Close one," Nancy says and laughs nervously.

"I'm supposed to be the clumsy one," Florence says.

"You are."

They start to row. From her seat at the back, Nancy steers and generates most of the force that propels them forward. Her strokes are long and powerful. Florence tries to keep pace, but she's much weaker. Every few strokes, Nancy corrects the canoe from drifting diagonally to the right—away from the middle of the lake. When they're about one hundred feet from the shore, Nancy stops rowing.

"Are you sure you want to go to the middle? It's a long way there and back. The cove is faster."

It's a sensible suggestion. The water in the cove is three feet at its deepest. They could walk out of the lake if their canoe collapses. They'd have to squelch through a ton of disgusting mud, but they've done it before.

"It's not deep enough," Florence says. "Plus, it smells

horrible. I hate making wishes in the cove."

"It's your wish," Nancy says, though Florence can hear the disappointment in her friend's voice. Then abruptly, she adds, "We need to paddle faster. You promised."

It takes twenty minutes to reach the mouth of the channel. As they row into the open water, a strong, steady breeze hits their back. The little canoe picks up speed, and Florence rests her aching arms. The wind is going to make it difficult to get back to shore, but right now, she's grateful for its help.

Ten minutes later, it starts to drizzle. The water is cool, and its touch sends goosebumps rippling across Florence's neck and down her bare legs. A moment later, the wind picks up. It's so strong that it wraps her thin hoodie around her body. *Nancy won't like this*, she thinks. Preemptively, she calls out, "We're almost there. Five more min—"

The canoe jerks diagonally to the left. Nancy is dragging her paddle in the water, using it like an anchor. Their momentum dies, but the canoe continues moving forward with the wind.

"It's raining and only going to get worse," Nancy shouts. "Make your wish here. Right now."

"We aren't far enough." Florence doesn't turn around. She shouts this over her shoulder. As she does, she dips her paddle in the water and redirects the canoe to the lake's center.

"Turn around and look, Flo. Actually look."

Squeezing her paddle tightly, Florence shakes her head. If she doesn't look, whatever is back there isn't real.

"Flo, you have to." Nancy's voice is high and angry. They've had arguments, but she's never sounded like this before.

Twisting to look, Florence inhales sharply. A wall of rain races toward them faster than they could ever hope to row. The lake water pulsates angrily from the storm's attack.

"Flo," Nancy says, color absent from her face, "you need to do it now. If we go any farther, I don't know if we'll be able to get back."

As Nancy finishes the sentence, the storm engulfs them, blotting out everything. Florence can barely see ten feet in front of her. Maybe less. Instantly, the boat and paddle are slick to the touch. Her clothes feel like they've doubled in weight. Florence knows this is bad, but they are so close to the center of the lake. She doesn't want to turn back. She can still make her deep wish. She can make her pain go away.

"A little more!" Florence shouts back.

"No, now!"

"It's not deep enough!"

"We're going to drown!" Nancy cries out, her voice on the verge of tears.

Florence's stomach drops. Nancy is the fun one, the extrovert—the danger seeker. It takes a lot to rattle her. *I've messed up bad.* Like Nancy said, Florence needs to make her wish now so they can row back to shore before the storm gets even worse. Before the canoe capsizes and spits them into French Lake.

"I'll do it here," Florence calls out.

She drops her paddle and digs into her pocket for the wishing rock. As she pulls the cream-colored pebble out, she fumbles it, and it disappears into the canoe's shadowy bottom. Leaning over, Florence runs her hands along the canoe bed until she finds it. *There you are!* She brings the wishing stone to her lips, kisses it lightly, and then shoots up, ready to throw it as far as she can. But her movement is too fast, too sudden, and the small boat is already rocking back and forth from the wind. She loses her balance for a second, but that's all it takes. She tilts to one side, and the canoe goes with her.

I've drowned us both, Florence thinks, and her mind becomes a jumble of thoughts. Did they bring life jackets? They don't always. They didn't, did they? She forgot to grab them when she went for the paddles. Florence squeezes her eyes shut and prepares to smack the water.

Something grabs Florence from behind and pulls her backward. She crashes hard into her seat. Nancy crouches behind her on her knees, her blonde hair plastered across her face. She must have scrambled across the canoe to stop Florence from tipping them into the lake.

Heart pounding, Florence hugs her friend. "Thanks," she stammers. She leaves the rest of what she's thinking unsaid. *You saved us!*

"Throw it hard!" Nancy shouts.

"Hard as I can. Just like you would." With Nancy

steadying her, Florence crouches awkwardly and eyes the lake's center. She pulls her arm back sidearm style so the rock will skip. "I want someone to love me," she shouts and throws. The rock cuts through the air and rain and slaps the lake water three times before disappearing into the storm's gray haze.

This is the best Florence has ever felt. Her wish will come true. It has to.

As the words pass her lips, lightning breaks the dark sky, illuminating the entire world for an instant. The afterimage burns in Florence's mind. They're surrounded by nothing but water. Menacing thunder cracks overhead. Florence's ears scream, and her stomach turns hollow. Somehow the rain starts to fall even harder.

"We need to leave right now," Nancy calls out. "We need to go fast."

◆ ◆ ◆

Clinching her teeth, Florence pulls hard on her paddle, putting every ounce of her minuscule strength into each stroke. Her heart pounds in her chest, rattling her body. Nancy's pace is grueling, and Florence's arms tremble and shake. This is impossible.

"I can't," Florence gasps and drags her paddle across her knees. She needs to catch her breath, to slow her heartbeat, to stop her arms and back from screaming.

Since the lightning strike, Florence has tried not to look at the lake. She's kept her eyes partially closed, so all she sees through is a little slit. But they've been rowing hard. They have to be close. They just have to be. She opens her eyes to see how far they've come and wishes she hadn't. They aren't even to the channel that leads to Nancy's house. They're still in open water. Behind her, Florence can sense more than hear Nancy continuing to row. Her friend's efforts are blunting the wind's impact, but the canoe is still being pushed away from shore. Despair washes over Florence, drowning what little hope she had left. *We're going to die, and it's my fault.*

Bending at the waist, she folds into herself and hugs her knees. She knows Nancy needs her help, that if they work together, maybe they'll get lucky and make it back to shore. But she's reached her limit. She's frozen in her own body, a broken promise with a heartbeat.

She is going to die tonight, in the cold, in the dark. There are a million places she wants to see—New York, L.A., Paris. A million things she wants to learn. Her mother was going to teach her how to make coconut macarons on Sunday. A life she wants to live. She was going to place an egg-shaped reading chair in her first apartment.

And what of her wish? It doesn't matter now. Florence is dead. Rita Baumgarten, Channel 10's evening reporter, a woman with puffy eyes and curly hair, will tell the world what happened. *"A developing story out of French Lake today. Two teens are dead after their canoe capsized during tonight's storm. It was Florence's fault, police say, because she felt sorry for herself and couldn't wait twelve hours for the storm to pass."*

Gentle hands grip Florence's shoulders and lift her up. With great care, Nancy leans into Florence's back, embracing her from behind. "It's okay," Nancy says. "I'm here."

"I'm scared," Florence says in a chatter that's on the verge of a wail. "I can't move."

"I know, but I can't do this myself," Nancy whispers. "I'm not strong enough. We have to row together."

Nancy's encouraging words don't help. Florence still can't move.

"Flo, I need you," Nancy continues. "I know you don't believe you can do it, but I believe you can. I know you. You're stronger than you think."

Florence bursts into tears, worse than anything she did early that day. She hugs Nancy's arms, which are draped over her shoulders. Even in the frigid rain, Nancy is improbably warm. She can't let her friend down. *You can do this.* She knows she can do it because Nancy told her she can. Florence hasn't broken her promise yet.

"I can keep going," Florence says.

"I know," Nancy replies and squeezes her tightly before clambering to her seat.

As they row, the canoe bounces up and down in the choppy water, catapulting them into the air. When they land, the boat seesaws wildly from side to side, and water sloshes inside. But miraculously, the canoe doesn't sink.

"Keep rowing," Nancy shouts, and Florence focuses on her friend's voice. The words fuel her.

Land appears through the gray haze. Florence doesn't recognize the shore, but it doesn't matter. *When we get back, I'm going to drink a gallon of hot chocolate. I'm never going to go onto French Lake again.*

Brilliant blue-white lighting blazes the dark, and thunder rumbles the sky. A cracking sound breaks through the storm's tumult. Along the shoreline, a massive tree bursts into flame. It's beautiful and terrifying. The unexpectedness of the lightning strike makes Florence scream and shudder. She loses her grip on the slick paddle. It slides gently into the lake like it wants to be there.

Panicking, Florence reaches for it. If she doesn't grab the paddle, the wind will blow it away. Then the wind will blow them away from shore. It's still too far to swim. Her middle finger grazes the oar, but she still can't quite reach. *Just a little more.*

"Stop," Nancy shouts. "You'll tip the canoe!"

Florence ignores Nancy and stretches farther. If she can reach the paddle, they'll live. It's half an inch away. Half an inch is nothing. *Almost, almost, almost.* She curls the tips of her fingers around the paddle and feels it move slightly toward her. "I have it—"

The canoe tips.

Water engulfs Florence. Rushes her lungs. Chokes her. She kicks hard and breaches the surface of the lake, flailing in all directions. She smacks an elbow against something hard and clings to it. It's the canoe. It's upside down but still floating. She tries to call Nancy's name, but more lake water invades her throat, and she gags. It takes her a few tries to spit it out.

"Nancy!" Florence finally manages to shout. "Where are you?"

"Help," Nancy moans from the opposite side of the canoe.

"Follow my voice. Swim to the canoe." She listens intently for the sound of someone swimming but can't hear anything over the rain. Moving carefully, Florence inches around the edge of the boat to where she thinks Nancy called out.

"Swim to me," Florence shouts into the gray.

Another burst of lightning flashes, and more thunder rumbles. The world flames bright. In this split second, Florence sees something floating in the water, but she's unsure what it is. She thinks she sees Nancy floating face down. *Swim to her. Pull her back to the canoe*, she shouts silently to herself. But she doesn't move. She can't. Her fingers are locked onto the canoe.

"Nancy," Florence calls out again. "Swim to me!"

It takes a long time for more lightning to rend the sky. When it comes, whatever Florence saw is gone, taken by the lake or the storm or both. She wails and grips the boat tighter. She shouts again.

"Nancy!"

Chapter Nine

Today

Nancy's house looks nothing like Florence remembers.

Twenty years ago, the Barnes residence was a muted yellow, with white trim around its windows and a baby blue porch. The lawn was lush and green and so soft that in the summer neither Florence nor Nancy wore shoes when they played outside. There was a young maple, skinny but tall, under which the two of them read and drew. In front of the porch was a small herb garden that was so fragrant it must have been magical. When Florence closes her eyes and remembers the house, her tongue tingles with the taste of fresh mint.

Now the once-great house on Tumner Lane has gone to seed. The vibrant yellow is gone, replaced with a pedestrian white, thick with grayish filth. Prickly crabgrass and spikey weeds cover the lawn. Where the beautiful garden stood is a row of stout evergreen bushes in need of a trim. Seeing the house drained of its life breaks Florence's heart; she wants it to be exactly like she remembers it—beautiful and perfect.

Florence sits in the car, drumming her fingers erratically against the steering wheel. She's parked across the street and has been for the better part of thirty minutes. She's turned the ignition on and off half a dozen times as her anxiety and fear battle with her need to confess.

Tears well in the corners of Florence's eyes, and she wipes them away with the back of her hand. This is too hard. Foot chases, gunshots, and even leaving Peter were trivial compared to what she must do. How do you drop your biggest secret onto a woman you haven't seen for two decades? How do you admit your failure?

I can't do this, Florence thinks, and then repeats the words out loud.

She turns over the ignition and the engine hums to life. A Top 40 station blares. Florence eases her foot on the gas and creeps down the block until she reaches an intersection and stops. A minute passes. Then two minutes.

"Just turn!" Florence shouts. She smacks the steering wheel hard enough that her palm stings. She's at war with herself. If Peter were here, Florence would be inside already. She's positive of it.

An SUV honks behind her. Its driver is a nondescript woman with brunette hair and glasses. When Florence doesn't move, the woman peels her vehicle around her and mouths, "What the fuck?"

What the fuck, indeed.

If Florence doesn't knock on Mrs. Barnes' door, she came all this way for *nothing*, she left Peter for *nothing*. This is her absolute last chance. The disease is nearing its final stage. Florence's body is howling to explode. It's today or never.

Florence rests her head against the steering wheel and closes her eyes. She sees Nancy's body floating in the water. She sees herself clutching the canoe, too afraid to rescue her friend. She's so tired of disappointing everyone. She's so tired of disappointing herself.

"Be like Nancy," Florence murmurs. *Fight any boy. Climb any tree. Be a giant.*

Florence jolts up from the steering wheel and slams her foot on gas. She zips into the intersection and makes a U-turn. The little sedan rolls over the curve and thumps back to the street. Before she can think, she pulls into Mrs. Barnes' driveway, throws the vehicle into park, and steps out of the car. For good measure, she chucks the car keys as hard as can at a storm drain across the street. They bounce once before sliding into the darkness.

Can't back out now.

Afraid of losing momentum, she jogs across the lawn and raps loudly on Mrs. Barnes' front door.

"I'm coming!" a familiar voice calls. A latch clicks from the other side of the door and a peep window opens. A woman's face fills the exposed space. "Can I help you?"

Florence trembles and inhales through her nose to stay in control of herself. "Mrs. Barnes, it's me…Florence."

Mrs. Barnes tilts her head. She examines Florence's

face, and her eyes go wide with surprise before narrowing into concern. Stepping back, she unlocks the door and opens it. Stifling a small gasp, Florence takes in the woman she's traveled so far to see. Mrs. Barnes bears only a passing resemblance to the young mother Florence knew as a child. Back then, Nancy's mother was sun-kissed and effervescent. Now, like her house, she's faded and diminished. Her blond hair has given way to a striking white, and her powerful body has gone thin and soft. Ignoring safety protocol, Mrs. Barnes moves to embrace Florence. "Sweetheart, what's wrong?"

"Don't touch me!" Florence pleads and jumps back. She stumbles awkwardly off the porch but doesn't fall.

Mrs. Barnes scrunches her face. Her reaction tells Florence all she needs to know. Everyone alive knows someone who's been infected. That's the price of living in this world. "How long?"

"Four days. Mrs. Barnes, we should go inside, before someone sees me."

Mrs. Barnes takes a tentative step backward and then another so that she can quickly slam the door shut. The color drains from her face. Florence hopes she doesn't have to tell the woman she killed her daughter on her front porch. It feels wrong, as if being outside makes Mrs. Barnes more vulnerable.

"Please," Florence says. "It's…it's important."

It's a felony to harbor an infected person. Florence knows what she's asking Mrs. Barnes to do. It's a big risk. Made bigger by the fact that the DPF likely knows where she lives and will come around asking questions.

Time slows to an excruciating crawl and Florence can see Mrs. Barnes struggle to decide. The tension is cut when a small silver car drives past. A man waves out the window and shouts a greeting but doesn't stop. Small-town life in action.

Mrs. Barnes relaxes. "Hurry up, then." She heads in first and Florence follows.

The inside of Mrs. Barnes' home is different than Florence remembers. When she was a child, it was filled with vibrant colors. Mrs. Barnes always seemed to be painting one wall or another. As Florence looks around, her heart breaks even more than it did when she first saw the exterior. The walls are a dingy white. *It's been a long time since anyone painted anything in this house*, Florence thinks.

"In here," Mrs. Barnes says and leads Florence to a wooden dining room table. "Can I get you anything to drink?" She doesn't wait for a response and disappears into the kitchen, returning with two glasses of ice water. She sets both down and takes a seat at the table, just out of arm's reach of Florence. "Why are you here, Flo?"

Florence sips the water to gather her thoughts, but she didn't realize how dehydrated she was and finishes the glass in one go. Placing the glass on the table, she searches for the right words to say. Her silence goes on too long, and Mrs. Barnes' shifts uncomfortably in her seat.

"Are you…feeling it now?" Mrs. Barnes asks. She still sounds like a mother. Florence supposes she always will be.

"No," Florence replies. She hasn't experienced any symptoms since the previous afternoon when she started to turn incorporeal while driving. She was lucky to catch it in time and pulled over. "But it's always there now, a deep ache."

"I'm sorry, Flo. You don't deserve this. No one does. So many people are gone." She shifts her gaze to her glass and starts to slowly rotate it in a tight circle using her thumb and middle finger. "Your parents?"

"Mom's been gone almost three years. I don't know what happened to my father. I like to think he's living off the grid in a safe community."

"They were good people," Mrs. Barnes says, still twisting her glass, obviously lost in her thoughts. Eventually, she leans forward and whispers, "Do they know? Are you being followed?"

"I don't know—I mean, yes," Florence blurts out. The room is hotter than it was when she sat down and she's nauseous. Her entire body is on edge. "The DPF knows I'm infected."

"Do they know you're here?"

"I don't know."

Mrs. Barnes takes a polite drink of her water. The ice clinks off the clear glass, filling the silence. Her hand quivers. She's scared and has every right to be. Florence is contagious. Inviting her inside her home could be a death sentence. For more than one reason.

"You can't stay here," Mrs. Barnes says, her gentle but voice firm. "I'm sorry, dear, but you can't. I don't even know why you would come here. Do you need money? I can give you a little. You can stay for a few hours. But you have to leave."

Florence nods along. In this world practicality and caution are a necessity. "Thank you, but that's not why I'm here."

"Why then?"

"Nancy," Florence says, her voice cracking.

"That was a long time ago. It happened and I've moved on. You should too."

"I can't," Florence says, already crying.

Mrs. Barnes stands abruptly. Her chair squeals across against the hardwood floor, making Florence wince. "I'm sorry, Flo. This is a bad idea. You need to leave. I won't call the DPF. But you need to leave, right now." She steps toward Florence to usher her out, but freezes. It's easy math. It's hard to shove someone out of your home when you can't touch them.

"I need to tell you what happened," Florence says.

"I know what happened. My daughter drowned."

"You don't know," Florence says. "There's no way you could know. You weren't there."

This stops Mrs. Barnes in her tracks. She sways and then rests a palm against the table to keep from falling. It's as if the few minutes Florence has spent with Mrs. Barnes has aged her. "What don't I know?"

"Sit, please," Florence says and motions to the chair. "I'll tell you and then I'll leave. You'll never see me again." *No one will.*

Mrs. Barnes eases back into her chair, keeping her eyes on Florence, as if she's come to Greenewin to hurt her. In a way, Florence has.

"I forced her to go out on the water," Florence says.

"She didn't want to go. She knew it would be dangerous, but I wanted to go. The storm came on so fast, and the wind was too strong. We tried to get back. You have to believe me. We tried. We really did." Florence pauses and takes a deep breath. "It was my fault Nancy died."

Mrs. Barnes doesn't speak, and Florence holds her breath. Florence is certain the woman is going to scream at her and demand she leave. Part of her wants Mrs. Barnes to curse her.

"Oh, Flo, dear," Mrs. Barnes says carefully. "You didn't cause her to drown. You didn't make it storm."

Florence's voice catches as she speaks. "You don't understand. I could have saved her. But I was too scared."

All these years later and Florence still remembers the feel of the storm-tossed water, the chill of the rain drops. "When I came up, I grabbed the side of the boat and held on. I told everyone that I didn't see her again." Florence shut her eyes; this was the most difficult part. "I lied."

Mrs. Barnes leans forward. Her eyes are red and glassy.

Florence continues before Mrs. Barnes can interrupt; she needs to get this out, all in one go. "It was dark. The rain made it hard to see, but I *could* see her. I was so, so scared. I froze. I wanted to help her. But I didn't. I should have gone to her. I should have saved...." Florence lets her thoughts trail off. "I'm sorry."

Silence takes the room. Florence holds her stomach with her right hand and waits for Mrs. Barnes to punish her. A dozen heart beats pass, followed by a dozen more. It's then Florence realizes Mrs. Barnes isn't going to reply.

She has no words to share at all, which is somehow worse than being shouted down.

"Goodbye," Florence says, standing. She hoped telling Mrs. Barnes her secret would make her feel better, but she feels no different; she's the same person she was when she knocked on Mrs. Barnes' door.

Mrs. Barnes rises. They face each other from across the table. "Florence, I—"

A rapping at the front door cuts her off.

Florence jerks her head toward the noise. "Are you expecting someone?"

"No. Stay here." Mrs. Barnes heads to the door and looks through its peephole. "It's a woman. She's wearing a DPF jacket."

"I shouldn't have come here," Florence says, panicking. She rushes from the dining room into the kitchen. There is a sliding glass door here that faces French Lake. She pulls short when she spots Jake, the DPF agent Peter hit with the baseball bat, creeping toward the door with his handgun drawn. She expects him to snarl, to want revenge on her for what Peter did to him, but his face stays neutral. He's a determined man.

"Don't move," he shouts in a stern voice, and hard tugs on the door's handle with his free hand. The doorframe jolts and shakes but doesn't open. It's locked.

Chapter Ten

Florence has put Mrs. Barnes in danger, just like she did to Nancy. Why did she think she could outsmart the DPF? She edges away from the back door, down the hallway, and into the living room. Mrs. Barnes is still at the front door, frozen in place.

"Open up," the woman on the other side bellows.

The sound of glass breaking comes from the opposite side of the house. Jake is forcing his way inside. Florence glances up the stairs to the second floor. "Is there a way out?" She already knows the answer. The master bedroom overlooks the garage. If Florence is lucky, she can climb out a window, jump off it, and run.

"Upstairs," Mrs. Barnes says. She bounds up the steps and Florence follows. Mrs. Barnes heads to the left at the top of the stairs, away from the garage.

"No, this way," Florence says, but it's too late. Mrs.

Barnes is at the opposite end of the house.

Florence twists mid-stride and bounces off a wall before regaining her balance. From the ground floor, she hears Jake moving through the house. She rushes past the stairwell and through the corner of her eye sees Jake at the bottom, gun drawn.

"Halt!" he shouts.

Expecting a flurry of rubber bullets, Florence closes her eyes and braces herself, but Jake doesn't discharge his weapon.

"It doesn't have to go down like this, Florence," Jake says. "I know you're scared. We can talk it out."

She doesn't listen to the rest. There's no need. What he wants is clear, and even understandable. Florence doesn't want to be understandable. How can anyone think straight when they know they're going to die? Death is abstract until it's right in front of you.

"In here," Mrs. Barnes says.

As Florence reaches the room, she stumbles. *Oh, God! Nancy's room!* She doesn't want to go inside. It'll be like walking into a nightmare. She looks back down the hallway. Maybe she can still reach the master bedroom. It's a good idea but impossible—there isn't enough time.

Florence darts inside Nancy's bedroom and Mrs. Barnes slams the door. She locks it and backs away. Panting, Florence straightens her back and glances at the lock. She and Nancy installed it themselves because they wanted more privacy. To this day, she isn't sure why Mrs. Barnes let them do it.

It's painful, but she tears her attention from the door

and scans the rest of the room. In her mind, Nancy's room is unchanged, a memorial to her dead friend. There is black and white photography on the walls. Nancy's frilly bed is still there, pushed into the corner. A million glow-in-the-dark stars pepper the ceiling.

The room Florence now occupies has none of Nancy in it. A wooden desk and computer are wedged in one corner next to a half-full bookcase. A twin bed hugs the wall across from Mrs. Barnes' home office. The room is cold and sterile and wrong—Nancy's memory has been stripped away.

Mrs. Barnes drops onto the guest bed and gasps for air, winded from the short burst of action. Grunting, Florence heaves the bookcase in front of the entrance. It's barely in place before Jake's heavy fists pound the door, causing Florence to jump back.

"Let Mrs. Barnes go, and we can talk about this," Jake says. "No one has to get hurt."

"Go away!" Florence shouts back, surprised at how angry she sounds. And she is angry, she realizes; angry at the shit hand she's been dealt; angry with herself; angry with everything.

"You can't escape," Jake replies.

Florence pulls herself away from the door and knells in front of Mrs. Barnes. "I'm sorry I got you into this," she whispers. She stammers before realizing what they must do. "You have to tell them I threatened you. Whatever they ask you, say that I threatened to infect you unless you helped me. You had no choice."

"You're going to turn yourself in?" Mrs. Barnes asks.

Florence nods and does her best to fight back more tears. She was so very close to accomplishing her goal. There's just one more thing she needs to do. "I have to. I didn't want it to end this way. I thought I had a little more time."

Mrs. Barnes looks at her quizzically and Florence is shocked the woman isn't angrier. In less than ten minutes, Florence has upended the woman's life. "What else do you have left?" she whispers back.

More pounding from Jake. "Kathleen, are you hurt? Are you infected?"

"Just a minute, please," Mrs. Barnes replies, voice quaking. "I'm safe for now."

"I want to ask Nancy to forgive me," Florence says in a low, embarrassed voice. "I was going to go to the lake."

Mrs. Barnes' face sags and her lips pull down. Her sadness is palpable. "Dear, she's gone. She's been gone a long, long time—you can't ask. She can't offer forgiveness."

Florence swallows hard. She knows Mrs. Barnes is right, but it doesn't change her desire for absolution.

"Flo," Mrs. Barnes continues, "she was my daughter and your best friend. She loved you like a sister. She'd forgive you if she were here. She wouldn't want you to hurt. I forgive you. She would too."

Florence lets her tears flow. She's waited years for this moment. Dreamt about it. But now that it's here, it feels hollow. The pain and anguish are still there; the weight of her mistake is still there. Nothing has changed. "Thank you," she utters, unsure what else to say.

Mrs. Barnes reaches out to touch Florence's cheek, to comfort her, but stops short. "What's wrong?"

"I feel the same. I thought I'd feel different."

Mrs. Barnes climbs off the bed, motions for Florence to make space for her, and then kneels in front of her. It's a slow process that shows Mrs. Barnes' age, and Florence can't help but think she's robbed the woman of her caretaker during her twilight years.

"Florence, I can forgive you. And I know Nancy would forgive you. But you have to forgive yourself. No one can do that but you. You have to let it all go."

"How do you stop caring?"

"You don't stop caring. You accept that you can't change the past."

"I don't think I can."

Silence fills the room. And then fire fills Florence.

It comes on all at once, a searing heat that roils through her flesh. At the same time, yellow-orange light illuminates every cell in her body. Hissing in agony, Florence arches her back and senses her shirt and pants crumbling to the floor. A thought cuts through the torment: *Protect Mrs. Barnes.*

She flings herself away from the woman, and as she does, she starts to rise off the ground like she did in the field. But something is different this time; the edges of her fingers are disintegrating into motes of light and floating away. Pushing away the fire within her, she grits her teeth and wills her body to be solid. It works, and she plummets to the floor.

"Kathleen, what's happening?" Jake bellows. "I need

you to speak to me!" He throws his shoulder into the door, but it holds.

"Don't come in," Mrs. Barnes tells him.

Florence wipes sweat from her forehead with the back of her hand. "I came all this way, and the answer was to look inward." She laughs; it's that or cry harder. "That's too *after-school special* for me."

"That doesn't mean it isn't true," Mrs. Barnes replies.

Florence lets Mrs. Barnes's words sink into her mind. She needs to prove to herself that she's changed. Prove to herself that she would save Nancy if she had the opportunity. Only then could she forgive herself.

Pain racks Florence once more, and she shudders as her body vacillates between corporeal and incorporeal states. Still worried for Mrs. Barnes, she careens to the far corner and holds her breath until the blistering heat subsides. *Almost out of time*, she thinks, gasping for air.

"Florence, are you alri —" Mrs. Barnes starts to say, but a loud *thwack* cuts her off as Jake once again throws himself against the flimsy door. He rams it a third time and then a fourth. The door bends, then cracks, spraying splinters into the room. His fifth strike breaks the lock, allowing him to shove the bookcase out of the way. With their handguns drawn, Jake and the older agent, Erin, ease into the room, their movements slow and precise.

"On the floor!" Jake says in a commanding voice that isn't exactly a shout.

It's over. Florence is finished and she knows it. She drops to her knees and raises her arms high above her head. As she does, a strong wave of regret crashes into her.

Then the gravity of the situation strikes her. Mrs. Barnes is pressed against the wall next to the twin bed. Her face is contorted in confusion and shock. She's in as much danger as Florence. "I didn't touch her!" Florence shouts. "She's clean! I swear it!"

Erin swivels her handgun to Mrs. Barnes. "Go to the opposite wall where we can see you. If you make any sudden movement, I will take it as an act of aggression. I will shoot you. Do you understand?"

Mrs. Barnes nods.

"I need verbal confirmation."

"I understand." She shuffles to the back wall so she's in line with Florence.

Satisfied, Jake returns his attention to his target. His face is stern and commanding. Florence wonders how many people he's executed in his career. Dozens? Hundreds? Will Jake even remember her face in a week? "Where is the man who was with you?" he asks.

Florence smiles. Jake asking about Peter is a small victory. It means the DPF hasn't found him. It means he's still alive and out there somewhere, living for them both. "I don't know. We split up."

"Where did you last see him?"

Florence lifts her chin. "I'm not going to tell you."

"Where is he going?"

"I don't know."

"Is he infected?"

She almost says "no" but instead she inhales the word. She has one last gift for Peter. "Yes, and he'll be dead soon, if he isn't already." She prays her lie will throw the DPF agents off his trail.

Jake doesn't reply immediately. His neck turns red and the vein in his forehead stands out. "Do you know how many people you endangered by running?"

Florence has considered it. She can't justify her actions, other than to say that this was something she had to do. "We were careful," Florence says meekly. "We didn't infect anyone else."

"I can't take your word for it."

Without taking his eyes off Florence, he says his partner, "Erin, do you want to pass judgment or should I?"

"It's your shoulder they hurt," she says decisively.

Jake squares his back and Florence knows what's going to happen next. The words are burned into her memory—just as they are burned into the nation's collective consciousness. "Under Section Thirty-One of the Public Safety Defense Act, I pronounce you guilty of knowingly endangering the lives of the citizenry of the United States of America. Your punishment is execution by lethal injection. Do you have a final statement?"

"You don't have to do this," Florence says. "I don't have much time left. You can wait."

"Do you have a final statement?" Jake repeats, stone in his voice.

Florence looks over at Mrs. Barnes; the color has drained from her face. "I'm sorry…for everything." Then she locks eyes with Jake. Her heart sounds like a cannon in her ears. She was so close to finishing it. "I'm ready."

As Florence stands, Jake steps back and holster his

handgun. He draws another weapon from his belt, a dart gun loaded with a lethal cocktail of chemicals. He points the weapon at Florence's chest. "May God have mercy on you," he says.

Florence closes her eyes and thinks of Nancy, thinks of Peter. She inhales deeply and waits for the dart to strike her chest. Then the disease renews its assault on her body and turns her into a raging inferno. Light erupts inside her, and she starts to vibrate uncontrollably. Every part of her body—her chest, her arms, her thighs, her face— breaks apart, comes back together, and then breaks apart again.

A loud pop echoes through the room, and a piercing sensation rips through her torso. She cries out and looks down—but there's no wound. The dart has gone through her. Florence focuses on her body and wills it to come together. It's like forcing hot air into a burst balloon.

"Shit," Jake stammers, and Florence realizes he's just as scared of her as she is of him. He raises his weapon to fire a second time.

"I have to do this," she says and throws herself backward into the wall. At the same time, she lets Solomon's take over. Her body convulses between states, and she passes through the wall into the afternoon sunlight. Once outside, she wills herself solid again and rockets to the earth. It's a short, painful fall. She slams into the ground on her back with a heavy thud and lays there dazed.

"Keep moving," she says to herself through clenched teeth and rolls over.

A jolt of satisfaction races through her. She's in Mrs.

Barnes' backyard. She can see French Lake.

Chapter Eleven

Florence drags her aching body upright and spots Mrs. Barnes' dock jutting into the lake. Of all the places she could die, it's the most fitting. It's her and Nancy's special place, where they shared their dreams and fears. It's where Florence felt safe as a child.

"It'll be over soon," she whispers and jogs toward it. With each step, the glow emanating from her body intensifies, and the fire raging inside her burns hotter.

She slows to a trot as she reaches the platform. Like the rest of Mrs. Barnes' property, it's a shadow of its former self. The wood is a sickly gray-brown and spotted with moss. The rope railings that were once vibrant blue are now frayed and pale.

Gently, Florence probes the rotten wood with her toes to see if it can take her weight. When nothing happens, she pushes harder, and the landing trembles and sways. It'll hold, but just barely. If she were heavier, the whole thing would collapse underneath her after a few steps.

"It's time," she says, steeling herself.

A sharp crack stirs the air, and something hard slams into Florence's back, knocking her forward. White stars explode across her vision as she smacks face-first onto the dilapidated wood. Underneath her, the structure rocks side to side, creaking loudly with each movement.

They shot me with a rubber bullet, she thinks, confused and outraged all at once. It's not fair. Other than running from the DPF, she's a good person. She was a school-teacher before the outbreak. People trusted her with their children. She's never even had a speeding ticket.

"Don't move!" Jake shouts from somewhere far behind her.

"Leave me alone!" Florence calls over her shoulder. She shoves herself to her knees and crawls. She needs to reach the edge before she gives in to the disease.

"You're making this harder than it needs to be!" Jake shouts. "I'm trying to help you. The injection is painless."

Against her better judgment, Florence glances back. Jake is at the shoreline now, holstering his firearm. He removes his dart gun and cocks it. He's knocked her to the ground so he can execute her.

"Why are you doing this?" Florence screams.

"I'm saving lives!" he replies. With his weapon raised, he takes a tentative step onto the dock and then a second and third.

"It won't hold us both," Florence says.

Jack raises his dart gun. "I can swim."

"Please, wait. It'll be over soon. I can feel my body breaking apart."

Jack frowns and shakes his head. "I have my orders."

Florence wants to scream. Why does it matter? There's no one she can infect. Why won't he let her have this?

"You should know that I don't take any pleasure from this," Jack continues. He narrows his eyes and aims.

Florence can't look, won't look. She turns back to her destination and keeps crawling.

As she nears the edge, a loud moan arises from the dock, followed by the sound of wood snapping. The front of the platform collapses with an anticlimactic splash. Florence's heart squeezes at the sight—it's like watching part of herself crumble.

"Shit," Jack blurts out, and Florence whips around to see what's happening. The back half of the dock, the section that touches the shoreline, has also collapsed, trapping them on the water. Jack is at the far end, arms outstretched, trying desperately not to fall. He lists to one side and then the other before catching his balance. "Almost," he says and raises his weapon again. "Look away. It'll be easier."

The dock shifts again, and the decaying wood under Jack's feet snaps. He topples forward, and Florence's stomach twists as the side of his head collides with a support post. He goes limp and slides into the lake on his back.

Instinctually, she scrambles for Jack to keep him from

drowning but yanks her uncovered hand back as she's about to touch him. She can't risk it. She might save him from drowning but infect him in the process.

Weighed down by his protective uniform and his traitorous muscles, Jake starts to sink. Florence's heart jackrabbits, and she whimpers, unsure what else she can do to save him.

"Wake up!" she barks and smacks the splintery boards underneath her with her palm. "I'm right here! You almost have me!"

Nothing happens.

Coming to her knees, Florence cups her glowing hands around her mouth and calls for help. Where is Jake's partner? Where is the stern-looking woman?

As she screams, more pain flows through her, and she locks up as if she's being electrocuted. Her body goes weightless and rises into the air. One foot. Two. Three. Five. The whole time, she keeps her eyes pinned on Jake's unmoving body. Guilt and fear mix inside her heart. Jake is going to drown like Nancy did all those years ago. Here's another person she could have saved if she knew how, if she was braver, smarter, better. Florence wishes Peter were here. She wishes Nancy were here. They'd know what to do.

But they aren't here—you are. You have to do it. There is no one else.

She sees Nancy struggling to stay afloat in the storm. She's replayed the moment countless times, but not once has she imagined what would have happened if she actually swam to her friend. Now, floating above another desperate person, she lets herself imagine a new ending. She lets go of the canoe. She swims to Nancy. She pulls her to safety.

"No, not again," Florence says to herself and, using the last of her will, forces her body back together, starting with her disintegrating hands. She concentrates on her fingers, pictures how they look and the sensation of running them through Peter's thick mane and holding Nancy's hand. As she does, the motes of light stop floating away and return to her. A satisfied noise—half gasp, half laugh—crosses her lips.

Then gravity takes her.

She crashes into the dock, and miraculously, it doesn't shatter into hundreds of pieces from the force of her impact. She's off her belly in an instant and searches for something—anything—that might help save Jack. All she sees are rotten planks, old rope, and Jake's dart gun. She can work with these.

She tears the rope railing from the remaining posts and gathers it up. Working quickly, she knots one end of the rope around the dart gun, transforming it into an anchor. She ties the other end to the bottom of the closest support post.

Gripping the gun tightly, she dives into the cool lake water so that she passes under Jake. She emerges a few feet past him and, with a small grunt, flings the weapon over him so that the rope wraps around his midsection. Then she repeats her swim in reverse, making sure to grab the weapon before she surfaces.

It takes all her strength to climb onto the platform.

Her body tells her to rest, to catch her breath, to pause, but she ignores it. Hand over hand, Florence pulls until the rope goes taut with Jake's weight. Gradually, his face and shoulders rise to the surface. As long as she holds the rope tight, he won't drown. As long as she stays solid, he'll stay alive.

"I can do this," she says on repeat, her muscles trembling from fatigue. She keeps going even when parts of her forearms float away, even when the top of her knuckles peel away.

Erin, the other agent, rushes out of the back door to the shoreline. Her face is as pale as moonlight. "Don't touch him!" She raises her weapon.

"If I let go, he'll drown," Florence gasps. "I can't pull him up. You need to swim to him."

The agent hesitates. "Did you touch him?"

"No," Florence says. "I'm trying to save him. Please, this is it for me. I can't hold on much longer."

The moment stretches, and Florence's grip on the rope slips. She growls and pulls harder.

"I'm coming," Erin says in a rush. She drops her weapon, kicks off her boots, and wades into the lake. When the water is deep enough, she dives and swims toward Jake.

Gritting her teeth, Florence strains and screams for Erin to swim faster in her mind. As she does, a convulsion strikes her, and she can no longer ignore the agony. Heat flares across every inch of her body. She is a guitar string ready to snap from too much tension.

Just a little longer, she tells herself. But her will is spent.

She's exhausted, and every second is a struggle. The self-ish part of her wants to let her body break apart and end the torment. Jake was going to execute her. He deserves to drown.

That's not who I am!

Yellow-orange motes the size of pebbles break free from her arms and legs. There should be blood from the missing tissue, but there's only light. "Oh, God," she stammers in shock and concentrates, trying to pull the light back to her—it doesn't work.

Panicking, she grips the rope tighter, and her right hand plunges through it and into the wooden boards below. Jake's face dips beneath the surface. Her mind flashes to Peter and all they went through to reach Greenewin. If he were here, he'd find an inner strength to keep going, to keep pushing. She can too. With a primal scream, she stands on trembling legs and uses her entire body to lift Jake's face out of the water.

Erin splashes forward and pulls Jake to her. "I have him," she shouts.

Florence lets the rope fall, staggers backward, and collapses onto her stomach. Her body writhes, and the terrible pain she's fought since her hand punched through Nancy's photo in the motel bathroom vanishes. She rises.

Twisting her hips, Florence rotates her body toward a cerulean sky. Luminous motes surround her. Her arms are gone to her elbows, her legs to her knees. The skin on her stomach breaks away, revealing a blinding light so beautiful it makes her cry.

"I'll see you soon, Nancy."

Epilogue

Peter freezes as he steps outside the farmhouse and exhales slowly, trying to calm his nerves. His palms are slick with anxiety, and he adjusts Florence's remembrance casket so he doesn't drop it. He knows Florence is gone, but having a funeral makes her passing somehow more real, more final.

A gentle hand rests on his shoulder from behind. "Are you okay?" Sam asks. "We don't have to do this now. We can wait."

"I'm fine," Peter says to his old friend. "I want to do this. The longer I wait, the harder it will be."

Sam doesn't reply but squeezes his shoulder.

"We're here for you, Peter," Missy, Sam's wife, says. "Take as much time as you need."

The three of them are on the back lawn. Ahead of them is a thriving flower garden, lush with tulips, daffodils, and hyacinths. The air is heavy with the sweet, honey-like scent of the flowers. Overhead, the sky is clear, and the sun's rays are warm against Peter's skin.

Straightening his back, Peter draws on his memories of Florence for strength. He remembers her smile, her freckles, the shape of her collarbone. He remembers the night the power went out during a storm and how they danced by candlelight to the patter of the rain. He remembers the last time they made love.

"I'm ready," he says in a low voice and starts the procession to the garden and the shoebox-sized grave he dug the night before. They go slowly and weave through the garden until they reach a maple-colored wooden bench Sam built in memory of Florence.

To the right of the bench is a small table with a pink pastel tablecloth and a framed picture of Florence. The sight of it makes Peter's knees weak, and he fights the urge to flee. She is so beautiful in the picture. Her wavy hair is loose around her shoulders, and she's wearing an oversized, floppy hat. *I should have said I loved her more,* he thinks.

When he reaches the grave, Peter sets the casket on the table and opens it, revealing a soft white lining. He chokes down a wail, and as he turns to face Sam and Missy, hot pain jets down his tender shoulder, causing him to hiss.

"Peter?" Missy asks, going into nurse mode, and not for the first time, he reminds himself how lucky he is to know her. When he arrived, his wound was infected, and he was half delirious.

"I'm okay," Peter says, raising a hand to stop her from

approaching.

As the pain subsides, he studies his closest friends. Tall and lean with dark skin, Sam is classically handsome, and his graying beard and round glasses give him a scholarly appearance. Missy is a petite Filipino woman with a kind, measured voice. The pair stand next to each other, gloved fingers intertwined. Seeing the two of them take comfort from each other drives a knife into Peter's heart. He'd give anything to hold Florence's hand again.

Pull it together, Peter thinks while fighting back tears. *This isn't about you.* Closing his eyes, Peter searches his mind for something to calm his nerves and deflect the despair eating his insides. He settles on a lyric from "White Van," a lesser-known song from The Midnight Provisionists' second album. *When you're here, be here. Don't chase tomorrow before living today.*

"We're gathered to remember Florence Wray," he says. "She was a lover, friend, and teacher. She carried one great regret in her life, and I'm certain she found forgiveness before she was taken from us. I invite you to place an object that reminds you of Flo in her remembrance casket."

Missy goes first. She carries a small arrangement of artificial flowers made from scraps of cloth and paper. Their petals are overly large and exaggerated. Florence would have loved them, not because of their uniqueness but because Missy used a tiny bit of her finite time on Earth to make them. "I'm sorry, Peter. She was a good woman."

"Thank you," Peter creaks.

Sam is next. He places a wooden apple he carved into the casket. "Florence loved her students more than any teacher I've known. She helped hundreds of kids and made the world better."

Peter dips his head in acknowledgment and waits for Sam to return to his place next to Missy before moving on. He doesn't want to continue, but he knows he must, even if it hurts his soul. Taking up the acoustic guitar, he strums it once and stops to collect himself.

"I wrote this song for Flo on our first anniversary," he says and then looks to the sky. "I hope this finds you." He starts to sing.

I've never been a smart man;
Learning doesn't come easily.
But for you, I'll be a student.
There are so many possibilities.

I know one hundred ways to love you.
Tomorrow I'll learn one hundred more.
I'll never stop learning to love you.
Every day, you'll teach me more.

That first night that we met,
I can't forget.
I loved everything about you:
Tousled hair and blue paint on your cheek.
I wanted to learn everything about you
To love you as you deserve.

I know one hundred ways to love you.
Tomorrow I'll learn one hundred more.
I'll never stop learning to love you.
Every day you'll teach me more.

Peter wipes his eyes after he finishes and removes Florence's orange engagement ring from his finger. He places it in the casket and closes the lid.

Appendix

Degenerative Incorporeality Timeline in the United States of America

Year One

February 17: Clusters of patients in Jacksonville, Los Angeles, Mesa, and New York City begin to experience intense burning, incorporeality, glowing, and weightlessness.

February 20: Dr. Nathan Solomon, director of the National Institute of Allergy and Infectious Disease (NIAID), holds a telebriefing to announce the name of the phenomenon—degenerative incorporeality—and warns the disease spreads through person-to-person contact. The public begins referring to the condition as "Solomon's Disease." Outside the United States of America, degenerative incorporeality is called the "American disease." Countries, including Canada, England, France, and Mexico, halt travel to and from the United States.

February 22: Paul Rodriguez, 59, a mechanic from Jacksonville, becomes the first confirmed death from the disease, disintegrating into balls of yellow-orange light. Medical professionals and scientists are unable to explain the phenomenon.

February 23: Cases of degenerative incorporeality are reported in Kentucky, Ohio, Wisconsin, and Virginia. Degenerative incorporeality is declared a pandemic. Dr. Solomon announces the origin of the disease is unknown.

February 24: States implement shutdowns to prevent the spread of the disease. King Village, Texas, becomes the first community to close its border to non-residents. Samuel Haywood, 19, a college student, is shot and killed entering the community to visit his girlfriend.

February 25: Democratic President Spencer Allen declares a national emergency. The Center for Disease Control (CDC) releases protective covering guidelines. When outside their home, people should wear head-to-toe clothing. Full-face masks are recommended but not required.

March 21: Riots and looting break out across the country from people frustrated with their lack of basic necessities and the Allen Administration's failure to provide government assistance. An estimated 20,000 people are infected with degenerative incorporeality.

April 7: The Allen Administration signs the Degenerative Incorporeality Safety Act (DISA) into law. The act includes funding for a one-time $1,000 payment per adult, expanded unemployment benefits, and rental assistance.

April 13: The Betterment Fellowship, a religious cult led by Rex Hambrock, purposely infects themselves with degenerative incorporeality believing the disease is a gateway to a "more meaningful and charitable world." Hambrock's manifesto is released on the Internet, sparking further purposeful infections across the country.

May 5: The Allen Administration announces gun deaths in the United States have tripled since the start of the pandemic.

June 23: Brittani Tighe, 30, a stay-at-home mother, becomes the first American to survive being infected with degenerative incorporeality. Dr. Solomon calls her survival an anomaly and reiterates the government has not found a cure.

August 14: Independent talk show host Alex Tribble, 48, a physician with a revoked medical license, announces he's discovered a cure for degenerative incorporeality. He directs listeners to purchase his "protective extract" on his online storefront.

September 1: At the behest of the Allen Administration, degenerative incorporeality survivor Brittani Tighe starts a ten-city tour of the United States to boost public morale.

September 3: Brittany Tighe's tour is canceled after a crowd forms outside her hotel in Indianapolis, creating a mass infection event. Tighe is unharmed.

September 22: Republican Florida Senator Gary Walker announces his bid for the presidency. Walker calls for a nationwide task force to "preserve America through personal accountability and the judicious enforcement of safety protocols."

November 4: Talk show host Alex Tribble is drowned in a bathtub filled with his protective extract. A note left at the crime scene calls Tribble a liar and peddler of false hope. The assailant remains unknown.

December 9: In a teleconference, Dr. Solomon says there is "no cure for the fantastical" and resigns from his position as director of NIAID.

Year Two

February 21: The Allen Administration opens Comfort Centers across the nation. People infected with degenerative incorporeality must report to the centers to mitigate the spread of the disease.

April 5: Far-right militants kill 22 infected people at the Des Moines Comfort Center. The violent assault sparks copycat attacks across the country, leading to the death of 114 infected Americans and 42 uninfected Americans. The percentage of self-reporting infected people to Comfort Centers drops by more than 60%.

June 1: New York City and other large metro areas announce non-essential employees will work from home indefinitely.

June 14: President Allen signs into law a universal basic income of $279 per week per adult and an additional $100 per child for 18 months, or until the degenerative incorporeality pandemic ends. Senator Walker calls the bill an attempt to buy votes.

September 5: Senator Walker's daughter, Kimberly, 16, is infected. She disappears four days later.

November 8: Senator Walker is elected President of the United States of America. He vows to punish those who contribute to America's decline.

Year Three

January 20: During his inaugural speech, President Walker calls for the nation to put aside fears of degenerative incorporeality and to return to life as it was before the phenomenon began. He also announces plans to form a taskforce dedicated to locating and capturing people infected with degenerative incorporeality.

May 24: The Disease Protection Force (DPF) is formed. The head of the organization reports directly to President Walker.

July 4: DPF agents are granted the authority to "humanely" execute people with degenerative incorporeality to mitigate the spread of the disease.

July 5: Kameron Jones, 29, a banker, becomes the first person executed by the DPF after refusing to self-report to a Comfort Center.

September 16: Independent investigative journalist Brent Rice exposes a pattern of excessive abuse and premature death at the Birmingham Comfort Center. The investigation reveals 34% of infected people are being executed for minor safety protocol violations.

November 12: Montana Governor Cindy Hart mobilizes the National Guard after violent and sustained fighting breaks out between new gated communities and longtime state residents.

Year Four

January 23: The Walker Administration ends the federal

state of emergency.

April 17: The U.S. Department of Commerce releases a report detailing America's failing infrastructure due to a lack of laborers. Federal and state highways are in disrepair, prolonging travel.

June 25: The Walker Administration ends federal college loans in an attempt to increase the labor supply.

July 14: Prome, a technology company and the second largest employer in America, offers loans to students in exchange for ten years of company service. Failure to complete a degree results in immediate loan payback. Almost seven thousand people apply for a loan within 24 hours.

August 20: President Walker signs into law a bill that gives new mothers $5,000 annually until the child reaches the age of 18. The bill also enters new mothers into a weekly lottery for additional money.

August 21: Ardent Pictures releases *The Family*, a propaganda film starring degenerative incorporeality survivor Brittani Tighe as Kate, a woman who wants a child but struggles to become pregnant. The Walker Administration partially subsidizes the film.

September 2: Congress expands universal income benefits in what is seen as an attempt to bolster President

Walker and his allies' popularity ahead of the midterm elections. Employed individuals working at least 24 hours per week at specified jobs receive an additional $1,000 per week.

November 6: President Walker's opposition gains a slight advantage in the House of Representatives, ending one-party rule at the federal level.

Year Five

January 4: In a televised interview, Dr. Linda Stripe, director of NIAID, says the government is no closer to finding a cure than the day the phenomenon started, and that the world must learn to live with the disease. In a spontaneous show of grief, New Yorkers gather on their roofs to cry together. The date is referred to as Weeping Day.

April 30: Virginian Connie Hatcher, 26, an outspoken critic of President Walker, begins a campaign to walk across America wearing minimal clothing. She brings with her a framed photo of her deceased son and husband. Her goal is to draw attention to the government's failed response to the pandemic and raise money to fight increased poverty. She documents her journey on social media.

June 10: Connie Hatcher reaches 60 million followers on Takit, a popular social media app. She is now accompanied by 150 to 200 anti-Walker protesters who join her walk for days and weeks at a time.

July 4: America Only, a militia with ties to rightwing politicians, starts a harassment campaign against Connie Hatcher with the goal of forcing her to abandon her walk. Militia members berate he over the death of her husband and son. Later that day, they block her path and surround her and her followers. Despite more than two dozen calls for assistance, local law enforcement refuses to respond.

July 7: Connie Hatcher is reported missing.

August 1: Armed anti-Walker protesters gather at Connie Hatcher's last known location. They start a march to the Pacific Ocean.

August 4: President Walker calls for counter protests. America Only is forced to flee their counter protest after being overwhelmed. Thomas Russo, the founder of America Only, is beaten and stripped naked.

September 1: Various news organizations share a leaked tape of President Walker requesting Thomas Russo's assistance with Connie Hatcher. He's recorded saying, "The nation would be grateful if you just took care of her."

September 27: President Walker and Vice President Trever Holler are impeached and forcibly removed the White House. Speaker of the House Stacey Cole, a Democratic Representative from Georgia, is sworn in as the next President of the United States.

November 3: Anti-Walker protesters end their march in San Jose. Their route is known as Connie's Trail.

December 2: President Cole walks the final quarter mile of Connie's Trail and delivers a speech to the nation. She vows to restructure the DPF and restore dignity to those impacted by degenerative incorporeality.

Acknowledgments

Cerulean Sky would never have been published without the love, support, and gentle prodding of my wife, Sarah. As unlikely as it seems, I finished the first draft of *Cerulean* a few weeks before COVID-19 hit the United States. I immediately trunked the novella, believing people wouldn't want to read a pandemic story as they lived through one. My wife convinced me to pick the story back up a few years later. Thank you, Sarah, for believing in Florence and me. You're my foundation—I love you.

This story also wouldn't exist without Stephen King's *The Stand*. I read the unabridged version in junior high, and I've been chasing the high I got from it ever since. If you haven't read the book, add it to your TBR pile immediately. You won't be sorry.

Thank you, Mom and Dad. Your love of music and film set me down this path. I miss you both terribly.

To Alex Woodroe, thank you a million times over for pushing me to build out the world in *Cerulean* and demanding that I write the flashback chapter. Your persistence and encouragement gave me the beating heart of the story.

Genre-straddling books can be a challenge to sell. Thank you, Robert Lewis and Polymath Press, for taking a chance on my horror, fantasy, and romance amalgamation.

To my fellow Scribblrs, Lauren B., Lauren S., Mathew, Micheal, Sam, and Steven, thank you for your advice and feedback on my writing. I'm so happy to have finally found my people.

I'd also like to thank my friends Melissa and Rachel for their sage medical advice. Without you, Peter would have perished long before he found safety.

My final acknowledgment goes to you, the reader. Thank you for supporting small presses. You're helping bring new voices into the world and making dreams come true. High fives all around!

About the Author

David Corse is a dark fantasy and horror author from the Midwest. His short story, "The Amassing Man," published by Gamut Magazine, won the 2024 Literary Nasties for Best Short Story. His long-form debut, "Mother is Coming Home," can be found in *Split Scream Volume 6* from Tenebrous Press.

When not writing, David co-hosts *Award Wieners*, a pun-filled podcast about Academy Award Best Picture winners. He is also a frequent guest on the *Movie, Films & Flix* podcast, where he chats about slashers, creature features, and ghosts. You can find him on Bluesky @itsmedavidcorse.

Also available from Polymath Press

Where the Pretty Things Rot
Henry Snider

Wherever light exists, shadows wait just out of sight. In those dark places Polymath Press brings you sixteen tales of terror by author Henry Snider.

Within this collection...

Honeymooners travel across Utah only to discover something ancient awakening, addiction separates a couple when one dark vice replaces another, a woman wakes in a serial killer's cage, a dimensional doorway to another world bleeds into our reality, Union soldiers find themselves hunted in the fields surrounding a Virginia plantation, Chicago firefighters are at ground-zero for a biblical apocalypse, and ten other tales to send your dreams to a darker place.

Also includes a special preview of Henry Snider's forthcoming novel, *Drive-In Feature*.

Ghost Girls and Rabbits
Cassondra Windwalker

Flush with the victory of winning the election as Alaska's first Athabaskan Senator, Noni Begay wakes to find herself buried alive. When her coffin lid opens, though, it's not to rescue but to six years of captivity, betrayed by the one person she trusted most. Escape will require not only all her strength but all the strength and stories of the ancestors she had until now imagined were only a useful device, an accessory she wore to win votes and social media followers.

Mary Nelson's only daughter, Ryska, went missing ten years ago, with no one but her mother to search for her. Having used up every favor and chit she has, Mary is willing to risk everything on one last ploy to save her daughter from the monsters...even if she has to become one herself.

A chilling psychological horror novel excoriating the epidemic of missing and murdered indigenous women and girls in North America, Ghost Girls and Rabbits is an unforgettable read perfect for fans of Scandinavian noir and literary horror, told by two fractured minds in the trappings of myths truer than mirrors.

Arithmophobia: An Anthology of Mathematical Horror
Edited by Robert Lewis

"Arithmophobia," *n.*: The fear of numbers or mathematics.

Whether you love mathematics or find it terrifying, this anthology of original tales of terror is sure to send a chill down your spine. With an unlucky thirteen brand new horror stories and a bonus poem in case any readers suffer from triskaidekaphobia, these pages combine the talents of some of the genre's most experienced award-winning practitioners of terror and some of the literary world's most promising new voices.

These stories tell us of strange and horrifying new geometries, crazed and violent mathematicians, sentient and malevolent numbers, and even some new mathematical twists on some classic monsters. You needn't be a mathematician to experience these new forms of mathematical terror, though students of the discipline might recognize some familiar names and ideas lurking in the shadows.

So pull up a chair, dust off your abacus and slide rule, and prepare to experience…

Arithmophobia.